TWISTED

DARK LEGACY, BOOK 3

NATASHA KNIGHT

Copyright © 2019 by Natasha Knight

All rights reserved.

No part of this book may be reproduced in any form or by any electronic or mechanical means, including information storage and retrieval systems, without written permission from the author, except for the use of brief quotations in a book review.

ABOUT THIS BOOK

My brother was right. I always wanted my own Willow Girl.

What happened on that island didn't break me.
It twisted me.
Corrupted me.
Made me into a monster.

Although, I guess it's true what she says. You can't become something that wasn't inside you all along.

This was always going to happen.
I was always going to take Amelia Willow.
History and destiny sealed her fate. Sealed both of ours.

For months, I've been waiting.

Watching.
Preparing.

And tonight, everything will change.
Because tonight, I'll collect my own Willow Girl.

*

Twisted is the third book of the Dark Legacy Trilogy. I recommend you read Taken and Torn before reading Twisted.

PROLOGUE
AMELIA

*H*e says that together they twisted him. Made him the monster he's become.

But you can't become something that wasn't inside you all along.

A tear drops to the sketchbook on my lap, the blob smearing the lead. I wipe it away with the tip of my finger and watch the stain spread to the edge of the page.

I can't seem to stop drawing that night.

The night when the Scafoni brothers stalked into our home and we were made to wear those rotting, disgusting sheaths and forced to stand on those ancient blocks as Sebastian Scafoni, first-born bastard, looked us over like we were cattle.

I can't stop drawing the look on his face when he saw Helena.

Even if she wasn't bound like she was, she'd have stood out.

She always thought herself the ugly duckling but she's the most beautiful of all. She's special. Always was. Different from us. And so much stronger.

Crap.

I swipe the back of my hand across my nose and listen to the sound of tears drop fat and heavy onto the page and this time when I lay my hand on the sketch, it's to smear the wet across like maybe I can wipe away that night. Rub it off the page. Erase it out of history like it never happened.

"Oh, now look what you've done," he says. His voice is deep and low, and I swear I can feel it as much as hear it.

He takes my hand with his gloved one and pulls it away.

"Ruined it."

I look at him. I finally make myself look at him.

"I hate you."

He grins. Shrugs a shoulder, his grip growing infinitesimally harder.

I glance at my palm—it's black from the pencil—and look down at the page in front of me.

He's right. It's ruined.

But it doesn't matter. I have dozens like it.

Hundreds.

Thousands.

I can't stop drawing that night.

Can't stop it from happening.

Can't stop the Scafoni bastards from walking into our lives, upending everything. Coming into our home like kings, like they owned the place.

Although, I guess they did.

They owned everything. Our house. Our land. Our parents.

My sister.

Me.

I force myself to meet Gregory Scafoni's dark eyes with their strange turquoise specks and wonder how I'd ever thought he was an angel.

My angel.

My savior.

When all he is, is the devil.

1
GREGORY

I've been watching her for weeks.

Following from the shadows. Always nearby.

Lurking, like a ghost.

And it's a good thing for her because I'm not the only monster on these streets. She seems to attract them like bees to honey.

Sweet, sweet honey.

She feels my presence. I know it.

I see it in the way she looks over her shoulder when she steps out onto the street. The way she scans every room she enters.

Even inside her borrowed apartment, she knows she's not alone.

Not safe.

It wasn't hard to find her. To arrange everything for her.

And tonight, after all the preparations, all the waiting, I will reap my own Willow Girl.

I choose a seat at the darkest corner of the bar, look at my phone for the signal that she's on her way, check my watch when I still don't have it.

But she'll be here. She has no choice.

The bartender appears with my drink. He gives me a nod of untrusting acknowledgment. I've become a regular of the hundred-year-old bar over the last weeks. It's one of the last that still allows smoking. I do enjoy a cigarette now and again, but even I hate the lingering stale smell and constant fog of smoke. I don't know what it is that's drawn her to this place.

Or maybe I do.

It's so opposite who she was.

Or who I thought she was.

I wonder if the night of the reaping broke her or if she was broken all along.

I check my phone again. Still, no message. I text Matteo.

Anything?

Nothing.

I swallow my drink. Signal for another.

The door opens then, and I swear every time she enters a room, something shifts inside it. Like there's a charge of energy, a wire, live and dangerous, sparking electricity.

It's almost palpable, that shift.

And I know in an instant how she slipped unnoticed past Matteo.

The bartender does a double take. He smiles.

She makes her way to her usual spot as he sets a drink in front of her.

I hear her quiet voice from here. See her hold up her hand, signal the number three.

The bartender raises an eyebrow and she tucks her hair behind her ear and nods. The tips of her fingers are black. She must have done it herself.

A moment later, three shot glasses are lined up and tequila poured. The most expensive bottle he has.

I smile.

In the months she's been away from home, she's changed. The docile, meek Barbie-doll is gone. Was she ever that? The darkness inside her, it's on the outside too now. She took care of that tonight.

She drinks the first shot, pushes one toward the bartender. He likes her, I can see it. He's probably the only guy in this place who doesn't look at her like he wants to eat her alive. Although he's also about eighty-years-old.

They clink the remaining two shot glasses together and throw them back. Again, she squeezes her eyes shut as she swallows the stuff. The old man watches her with the tenderness of a father, and I think she just ordered another round because he's hesitant.

But she insists, and she always gets her way.

It's how it is with beautiful women.

Men drop to their knees to worship them.

The thought makes my jaw tighten.

I did it, didn't I?

I knelt.

I worshipped.

The whiskey tastes bitter as I swallow it down.

She picks up a few of the bar napkins and the pencil the bartender has already put in front of her. She never seems to remember to bring her own. I know she has better pencils. Sketchbooks full of the image she'll draw tonight.

Again, and again, the same one.

Hell, she's as obsessed as I am.

She starts, almost absently sipping on one of the shots. She rubs her right eye with the heel of her hand. Checks her watch.

I know what she's waiting for.

Who she's waiting for.

And it's time for me to make my move.

I slide off my barstool and make my way toward her. Her pencil pauses, and again, she pushes black hair behind her ear, and I see how she shifts just her gaze, peering at me from the corner of her eye.

The old man sees too because he's suddenly closer, wiping off a glass, eyes narrowed on me.

He's protective of her.

I'm glad.

He's been my ally for the last few weeks and he doesn't even know it. Because I've been protective too. I've been beating the monsters back. I'm not the only predator in town.

Her pencil is moving again, but her back has gone rigid.

I take the seat beside hers, angle my body toward her. I put my boot on the foot rest of her stool and lean in to peer at the napkin and when I inhale, I smell hair dye and her.

"I think the lady prefers to be alone," the bartender says.

I don't bother looking at the old man. Instead, I meet Amelia Willow's spectacular blue eyes and in that instant, I know she knows who I am.

I know she has not a single doubt.

"I like what you did with your hair," I say, pushing that same, disobedient lock back behind her ear, feeling her shudder as my gloved hand touches the smooth skin of her cheek.

My gaze falls to her mouth, glossy, pouty lips parted in surprise. I think how I'd like to kiss those lips.

Sink my teeth into them.

I look at the choker around her neck. A simple piece of black ribbon to match her newly dyed dark hair. The collar of her oversized sweater is wide. I push it over a little, watch it slide off her shoulder to reveal a red bra strap.

And when I put two fingers over her pulse, I feel the rapid drumming of her heart.

"Now look here," the bartender starts.

I meet her eyes again, smile.

She's still watching me, her eyes still wide. I can hear her breathing. It's a shallow, trembling breath.

"I said the lady prefers to be alone," the old man says again.

"Do you prefer to be alone, Amelia?" I ask her, never taking my eyes from hers, sliding my fingers over her delicate collar bone to the hollow just beneath her throat.

She tries to speak but has to clear her throat to get the words out.

"It's fine, Bobby," she says, a slight tremor in her soft voice. She never takes her eyes off me. "I know him."

2

AMELIA

I've known someone was following me for weeks.

Without looking away, I crumple the napkin, leave it on the bar.

Everything will change tonight.

It's what I want, isn't it? Why I'm here.

His fingers on my throat, they're gloved, but I swear I can feel the heat of them on me. He's sliding them back over my collarbone, his touch soft, and I know what he's doing. He's letting me know he can feel how fast my heart is beating.

"You sure, Amy?" Bobby asks. "I'll ask him to leave—"

"No." I turn to the bartender. He's sweet, he's been super sweet to me. "It's okay. I mean it."

"Yeah, Bobby, it's okay," Gregory Scafoni says.

I know it's Gregory and not Ethan. I have no doubt.

Maybe it's the gloved hand that gives it away. Helena said he'd hurt his hand. But she wouldn't tell me more. She never told me more.

I look back at him. He's as beautiful as I remember. Why is it the monsters are always so fucking beautiful.

"Don't be rude to him," I tell Gregory, my words independent of my thoughts.

Gregory grins, picks up one of the shot glasses, the one I've been sipping from, and nudges the other toward me with the bottom of his glass.

I pick it up.

He clinks his to mine and swallows the contents.

I do the same, already a little tipsy from the previous two but needing the burning sensation. The numbing effect of liquor.

He sets his empty glass down, picks up a handful of stale peanuts and throws them into his mouth. I watch him chew while he watches me.

His fingers smooth a lock of my new shorter, darker hair. I cut it tonight. I took the kitchen scissors and cut away almost ten inches, so it now falls to just above my shoulders. A sort of metamorphosis. The beginning of one.

I'm sure it's uneven but I don't care.

The color too, there are still smudges of black at

my temples, on my fingertips, on the ruined bathroom towels.

Going from blonde to black is a stark change.

But I'm different now, too. Starkly so.

Or maybe I've never been who I was supposed to be.

"It suits you," he says, meeting my eyes again. "Better than the blonde."

"You don't know me. How can you know what suits me?"

He smiles.

"Was it you?" I ask.

"Was what me?

"Following me?"

He nods. "You should be grateful. You attract the less than desirable sort."

"Like you?"

His smile widens, turns into a smirk.

I exhale loudly, shift my gaze to the empty glasses. I look up at Bobby, but he shakes his head no. He's leaning against the back of the bar, arms folded across his chest. For the first time since I've known him, I realize for as old as he is, he can probably take most of the men in here.

And he doesn't like this one.

I turn back to Gregory.

He types something into his phone and tucks it into his pocket and I notice how he's only wearing the glove on one hand, not both. I think it's strange.

But tonight isn't the night for this. For him. Tonight, I pay back the generosity of the woman in whose apartment I've been squatting.

Generosity. I dismiss the word.

I am an idiot.

The door opens and I turn to look to see if it's her come to get me, but it's not. It's a man and he's dressed in a dark suit, and stands just inside the door, hands folded together and I'm pretty sure I've seen him before.

"I need another drink," I say to Gregory.

He turns to Bobby and when the old man still won't get us more tequila, Gregory leans over the bar to take the bottle and pours us each a shot.

I see Bobby's hands fist, but he's seen the man at the door too.

When I pick up the glass, my own hand is trembling so hard that some of the tequila splashes onto the bar before I can get it to my lips to swallow it.

"You're not what I thought," he says.

"What did you think?"

"A beautiful bore."

Silence. I have nothing to say to that.

"What do you want?" I finally ask.

"A lot of things. Everything."

"What do you want with me?"

He grins. "A lot of things. Everything."

The door opens then and this time, it's her, the

woman I've been waiting for. Charlie's with her and when they see me, their mouths fall open.

It's the first time in days that the smile on my face is real because fuck them.

After a moment, the woman narrows her eyes and Charlie gives me a sorry look. I don't buy it though. He set me up. He pretended to be my friend and set me up.

"Friends of yours?" Gregory asks.

I turn to him, look at him in profile, at the sharp cut of his jaw, the dark scruff along it, a few days' growth.

His man at the door tucks a hand inside his jacket but Gregory gives an infinitesimal shake of his head and he drops his arm to his side.

"Not friends, no," I say, sliding off my bar stool to stand as they approach.

Gregory stands too, and I look up at him and I think I got him wrong in the sketches. His features, those are exact, but the darkness that clings to him, I didn't capture that.

I was too busy making a devil out of Sebastian Scafoni.

Charlie and Madam Liona stop a few feet from us.

"What happened to your hair?" she asks.

"I dyed it."

"I see that. Why the fuck did you do that?"

"Who the fuck are you?" Gregory asks.

They both turn to him.

I put my hand on his forearm. I mean to stop him, but for a moment, all I can do is feel the steel of it, of his strength. Absorb the strange energy rolling off him and into me.

He doesn't shift his gaze from them. Is he standing up for me? Defending me from them? He's not my ally or my friend or even remotely on my side.

Madam Liona turns to face him.

"I'm the woman who owns your girlfriend."

Gregory steps toward her, and for the first time since I met her, she shrinks away.

"Do I need to call the police?" Bobby asks from behind the bar.

"No, Bobby, it's okay. We're leaving," I say, without looking back.

"Amy," he calls out.

I turn to him. I try to smile but feel the tears building that I refuse to shed. "It's really okay. I'll be okay."

Will I though?

Charlie checks his watch. Whispers something into Madam Liona's ear.

"You own nothing," Gregory says like the whole conversation with Bobby hasn't been happening at all. "Your name."

She flounders, another first, and I look at

Gregory, at his back. At how big he is. How scary I know he can be.

"I'm Madam Liona."

He nods, steps backward, adjusts his cufflinks. "What's her debt, Madam Liona?" he asks casually, not even looking at her.

"None of your business," she says. "No need for a white knight, though you don't quite seem like one anyway. She's bought and paid for." She turns to me. "We'll discuss the hair," she says, gripping my arm, readying to drag me away.

The instant she does, Gregory's hand clamps over her wrist and I see from her face that it hurts.

"Thing is, she wasn't ever up for sale," he says.

Again, Madam Liona is flustered.

Gregory forcefully pulls her hand off me but keeps hold of it, twisting her arm a little as he steps between us, almost shielding me from her.

"But I'm a business man. Tell me the exact conditions of the transaction."

"It's not a negotiable—"

"The terms."

When she doesn't answer right away, he twists a little harder.

"Virgins are hard to come by. Especially ones that look like her. My client has bought all three virginities."

I feel a flush creep up my neck. I don't dare glance back at Bobby, I just hope he hasn't heard.

Gregory doesn't look at me. He already knows this. My sheath wasn't marked, only Helena's was.

God, the humiliation.

"What did he pay?" he asks casually, like this is the most ordinary conversation about the most ordinary of transactions.

She says the number, a ridiculous amount of money.

"Although, he's expecting a blonde."

"Well, that's too bad for him, isn't it?" He releases her wrist with a shove that puts her a few steps farther from me.

The man at the door steps forward now.

Gregory turns to Charlie. "And you are?"

Charlie's gaze falls on me, then back on Gregory and when he steps backward, he runs right into the other man who is twice as tall and a hundred times meaner looking. Charlie lets out a decidedly feminine scream.

From behind me, I hear the cocking of what I know is a shotgun.

"That's enough," Bobby says. "Amy, get over here. Behind the bar with me. The rest of you trash get the hell out of here before I put a hole in one of you."

Gregory turns to him his expression exactly the same as if having a shotgun pointed at him is the most normal thing.

"Noble of you," he says. He reaches out, touches the nose of the shotgun with the tip of one gloved finger and tilts it toward Madam Liona. "Aim for her."

"Fucking bastard." Bobby says but Gregory's man cocks the revolver he's now holding by his side. I get the feeling he's much more experienced with it than Bobby is with that shotgun.

"Here's what's going to happen," Gregory says. "I'm going to double what that asshole paid for the girl. You're going to get in your car and disappear and you're never going to come near her again. Is that clear?"

"What?" I ask.

Gregory turns to me, his expression cold. He raises his eyebrows.

"I don't..."

I swear he rolls his eyes just then. "I may be a devil but I'm the devil you know, sweetheart."

I swallow.

He grins, turns back to the woman.

"Double?" Her greedy eyes widen, she's already doing the math.

"Matteo," Gregory says.

The man with the gun steps forward. "Put her in the car. Wait with her." He turns to me. "She has a habit of disappearing."

Without a word, the man has his hand wrapped around my arm and is pulling me away.

"Wait!"

They all turn to me.

"I didn't agree."

"I wasn't asking if you agreed. But if you'd rather be fucked by a stranger tonight..." he trails off. He turns to Liona. "How old is he?"

"Uh...sixties."

Gregory shifts his gaze back to me. "You'd rather have to suck off a sixty-year-old fat fuck?"

I feel the blood drain from my face.

"I didn't think so."

He gestures to Matteo who resumes walking me out.

"But..." We're outside before that 'but' is acknowledged and a moment later, I'm in the backseat of an SUV with tinted windows and the man, Matteo, is standing beside the locked doors.

My coat is still inside. My purse too. Which is where my phone is.

Although, who would I call? The police? Helena?

Not five minutes later, Gregory walks out carrying my coat and purse. He opens the door and climbs into the backseat with me. Matteo takes the driver's seat and starts the engine.

"Buckle your seatbelt." Gregory unzips my purse.

"What?"

He looks at me. "Buckle your seatbelt. It's the law." He gives me a smirk that tells me he could give a fuck about any law.

But when I don't move to do as he says, he mutters something under his breath and reaches across me to buckle the belt before resuming his search inside my purse.

"What are you doing? That's mine."

He takes out my cell phone, opens the back and removes the battery before tucking both into his pocket.

"Now it's mine," he says. "Just like you."

He finds my keys and takes those as well.

We pull up outside the hotel where my apartment—Madam Liona's apartment—is.

"Stay here, Matteo. We'll be right back." He turns to me. "We need to get your things. You won't be coming back here."

"I don't understand what just happened," I say as he opens the door to step out.

He sighs, like maybe he's talking to someone slow, and closes the door. "You owed that cunt money and I paid it. In return, I bought what you'd already sold. Which is disappointing to hear. I thought you'd have more respect for your body, Amelia."

I know he's laughing at me. I can see it on his face.

"Fuck you."

He smiles wide, wide enough to bare his perfect, white teeth.

"I will fuck you," he says. "That's the point of this transaction."

"Can't get laid the old-fashioned way?" I don't

know why I ask it.

He scoots in closer, the smile vanishing, replaced by something darker, more predatory, more premeditated. He grips a handful of hair at the back of my head and tugs, making me cry out.

I slap my hands against his chest to push him off, feel the hard muscle there. I'm no match for his solid strength.

"Learn this now, Amelia Willow. I own you. And I won't let you go until I've had my fill of you."

He twists his fingers in my hair.

"Madam whatever the fuck her name was was right about one thing. I am no white knight. I am not your friend. I didn't do this out of the goodness of my heart. You and me, this was always going to happen. Destiny and all that bullshit." He pauses, cocks his head to the side. "And you know what? I don't think you're going to fight me."

"I will fight you."

He snorts. "I've heard those words before."

Before I can ask what he means, he tugs my head back hard and it takes all I have not to cry out in pain.

"Now be good or I'll have to really hurt you."

3
GREGORY

She doesn't give me any trouble as we walk through the lobby and ride the elevator up. It's coming though. I can feel it. My guess is she's still processing what just happened.

I watch her reflection on the mirrored elevator doors, her delicate skin looking even more so for the dark hair. This change, it's only made her more striking.

"Why black?" I ask.

"What?" she asks as if she's lost in her thoughts.

"Your hair."

She shakes her head dismissively. "I was tired of looking at myself. Tired of looking like them."

"Your sisters."

"You're a genius," she says with a smirk as the elevator doors open.

I grin, tighten my grip on her arm. "I'm going to

let that one go."

We walk down the hall to her apartment, and I insert the key into the lock.

"Wait," she starts when I push the door open. "How do you know which one is mine?"

"I already told you. I've been watching you for weeks."

"Why? I don't get why?"

We go inside, and I release her after closing the door. I dig my hand into my coat pocket and pull out the napkin she'd left on the bar. It's crumpled, but it's the same thing she's been sketching forever.

"This," I say.

She recognizes it, tries to take it from me, but I pull it out of reach.

"You've been leaving them like calling cards."

"You're collecting them?" she asks.

"I don't like to waste good art. You're very talented."

Her forehead wrinkles and her eyes narrow as she studies me.

"It's polite to say thank you when someone pays you a compliment."

"Keep your compliments. You mean nothing to me."

"I don't think that's true." I check my watch. "You have ten minutes to collect what you need."

"What do you mean?"

I raise my eyebrows. "I mean pack what you want

to take."

"Not that part."

I knew what she meant. It's just easy to fuck with her because I think I know something about her.

"You're as obsessed with it as I am, Amelia."

Concern deepens the blue of her eyes. I realize there's a fine gold ring circling the pupil.

"Obsessed with the reaping. The Willow Girl Legacy. Maybe you even find something romantic about it."

She snorts. "There's nothing romantic about what your brother did. How he did it."

"No?" I walk ahead of her into the bedroom.

She follows close behind.

I go directly to the table where notebook upon notebook is stacked all containing sketches. I open one, thumb through the pages, do the same with another, then another.

"Have you been inside here?"

"Now you're catching on."

"How?"

"Money. Money will buy everything." I cock my head to the side. "Even you. It bought your sister, too. Or do you forget how easily Willow Girls are bought and sold?"

She drops to the edge of the bed and I'm not sure if it's her new hair color making her look paler or what I said.

"Time's a ticking, Amelia." I close the books. "I'll

wait in the other room."

"I'm not obsessed," she says when I'm at the door.

I stop, turn.

"I just don't understand it. I don't understand how I feel," she says like I might have the answer.

"Like you want it?"

She snaps her gaze up to mine and what I see inside her eyes, I know I'm right.

"I don't want it," she denies.

I raise my eyebrows. I'm not interested in wasting my time with this conversation. I tap the face of my watch and leave the room to sit on one of the chairs as I wait for her. I check inside my pocket for what I need when she gives me the trouble I'm expecting and study the art on the napkin.

This one is slightly different than most of the others. In this one, she's pictured me, not Sebastian. It's incomplete, so I don't know which Willow Girl is standing on the block before me, but I can guess.

And it makes this all so much more interesting.

A few minutes later, she comes out of the bedroom with a backpack over one shoulder and a duffel bag in her other hand. When I move to take the duffel from her, she tugs it away.

She stops at the safe and punches in her code to unlock it. From inside, she retrieves her passport.

"I'll take that," I say, relieving her of it before she can argue. I tuck it into my pocket. "Let's go."

"Where?"

"Home."

She seems confused by that and stops, turns to me. "Is this for real?" she asks. "I mean, what you did, what you...bought...It's not legal or anything. I don't have to go with you."

"No, you don't. But I can make you. If it's part of your fantasy, I mean, to be taken by force—"

"What? No! God."

I chuckle. "I'm just having some fun with you. I do have one question, though." My smile is gone. "Are you going to give me any trouble?"

She steps backward, closer to the door.

"You mean am I just going to walk out of here with you? Get in the back of that SUV and let you kidnap me?"

"Yeah, exactly that."

"You bet I'm not, asshole!" She swings the duffel at me, and what the fuck is in it, stones?

I shove it away, pounce as she reaches for the doorknob, one hand clamping over her throat, pinning her against the door. I'm easily faster than her, stronger than her, and truly, it's better this happened here than down in the lobby.

But what I'm not expecting is a fucking knife at my throat.

"Let me go you sick fuck!"

She digs the tip of it into my neck, breaking skin.

But the instant she sees blood smear the knife's

edge, she freezes, her eyes widening in panic. She's too scared to do more and it's the split second I need.

"My bad," I say, squeezing her throat, closing my other hand around her knife hand and twisting it backward until she lets out a cry and the knife drops to the fake-wood floor.

"A fucking steak knife?"

"My...arm."

"Where the hell did you get it? Do you sleep with a knife under your pillow?"

She makes a gurgling sound and her face is pink.

I ease up on her throat. I don't want to kill her. But the instant I do, she's clawing at me with her free hand and when I capture that, she slams her knee into my balls.

"Fuck!"

I double over and the instant I let her go, she tries the door again, but I've double locked it and when she pulls it open, it catches on the hook.

I lean against it, slamming it shut and tackling her to the ground, my balls on fucking fire. I lay my weight on top of her as the wave of unbearable pain passes and I recapture her wrists.

"That was a mistake, Amelia," I say through gritted teeth.

It fucking hurts like hell.

She tries to free her legs probably to break my balls, but that's not happening. No fucking way.

"I knew this'd go this way," I say, reaching into

my pocket to take out a syringe. "But don't worry, I'm prepared."

She stops struggling when she sees it, her eyes growing even wider. "What is that?" she asks, restarting her effort, trying to get free of me.

But I've got her.

And I'm not letting her go.

I pull the cap off with my teeth and spit it aside. "Muscle relaxer," I say with a smirk. "Sort of."

"Don't!"

"You'll have a killer headache tomorrow, but you earned that."

I pull myself up, keep her trapped between my thighs and squeeze the air out of the needle.

"No, no. Please don't! Please. I'll go with you. I will!"

"Too late, sweetheart." Using my arm, I force her face to the side glad for the shorter hair. "Now be still."

"Please!"

But it's too late for her. I push the needle into her skin and watch her squeeze her eyes shut as I empty the contents of the barrel into her.

She makes a sound, and when I sit up and let go of her, she rolls her head to look at me.

"Next time be smarter," I say.

She blinks, struggling against the drug and tries to bat at me once, twice, but her arm just flops to the floor.

I take her hand and stand, ignoring the pain, pulling her limp body up with me. I hoist her over my shoulder and dig my phone out of my pocket to call Matteo.

"Change of plans. Meet me at the service entrance."

He chuckles. I guess we both knew how it'd go.

"Be there in a minute," he says.

I unzip her backpack, look inside. The notebooks. She wouldn't run without them. Zipping it, I pick it up and sling it over my free shoulder, leave the duffel where it is and give her ass a slap for good measure before hobbling out the door with as much dignity as I can muster.

I can't take the fucking elevator with her passed out over my shoulder like this, so I find the stairs and climb down fourteen floors.

Fourteen fucking floors.

Well, thirteen technically, I guess.

Maybe there's some truth to thirteen being unlucky. It was for her.

The coast is clear until I get outside where I pass two of the kitchen staff smoking. Matteo opens the back door of the car and I give the men a smile.

"Never knows when to stop," I say to them, suggesting she's passed out drunk.

They seem confused about what to do, but I don't care. I have her loaded into the back of the SUV and we're driving away before they can think.

4

AMELIA

I saw a movie once where these gangsters had this guy's head in some sort of vice-like device, and the guy was screaming as they cranked the jaws tighter, cracking his skull, literally squeezing his brains out of his ears. It was disgusting, and I couldn't look away.

That's what my head feels like right now.

"Morning, sweetheart."

My ears are slow to absorb the words, to place the man they belong to.

To remember.

We're moving. I can feel the vibration of being in some sort of vehicle.

My face is resting against something cold but when I try to lift my head, I think it's going to explode.

I groan.

He laughs and my head bounces against the cold, hard thing. Glass.

"Wakey, wakey. You're missing the best part."

I pry one eyelid open at a time because it's like they're glued shut. I raise my arms, and they feel heavy, like dead weights, but I rub my eyes, and when I open them, I see the deep orange glow of a sunrise through dense trees.

The car hits a pothole, jolting me into the man sitting beside me.

I gasp, bouncing off his hard body, and I turn to him and fuck, it's real. Last night. Madam Liona. Charlie. Him.

Gregory Scafoni.

It's all real.

"What did you give me?"

He wipes a gloved hand over the corner of my mouth, and I think I was drooling.

"Muscle relaxer. I told you."

A car passes opposite us on a road that seems way too narrow for two cars. It's lower than ours. We're in an SUV. A different SUV than the one from last night though.

And the passing car's license plate, it's different too.

A narrow, long rectangle in blue and white with an *I* and a circle of gold stars. Panic has me pressing my nose to the glass to see the disappearing car, trying to make out the license plate because it's not

American.

"Where are we?"

He chuckles. "Relax. Christ. You're so uptight."

I turn to him and a wave of nausea has me covering my mouth.

"Shit. Stop the car," he orders, and we come to a screeching halt and he just barely has me outside before I vomit along the side of the road.

I'm doubled over. He's holding me around the middle and one hand has my hair—or most of it—and we're standing in about a foot of snow.

"Where are we?" I ask again, but another wave hits and I puke again. "What did you do to me?"

After a few minutes, I straighten, wiping the back of my hand over my mouth, tasting bile.

The driver comes around, hands Gregory some sort of rag that Gregory uses clean my face.

"Done?" he asks.

As if I can control it.

"Get her some water," he says.

The driver reaches into the car, takes out a bottle of water, opens it.

"Rinse," Gregory says, handing it to me.

I do because my mouth tastes gross, but water isn't going to get that taste out.

I feel another wave but there's nothing left. And when he puts me back in the car, I don't fight. I don't have any strength to. I just let him strap me in and sit there, feeling gross and cold because my feet and jeans are wet from the snow and my head throbs and I can't get the taste of vomit out of my mouth.

"My head hurts."

"Learn a lesson."

I glare at him. "I hope your balls hurt as bad as my head."

"There she is," he says with a chuckle as we resume driving.

"Where are we?"

"About forty-five minutes outside of Rome."

"Rome?"

He nods.

I look outside again, read an unfamiliar traffic sign—a red circle with the number eighty in the middle. A speed limit?

"Rome?" I ask again.

"These are the outskirts. We're not in Rome proper."

"How?"

I was passed out. We'd have to have taken a flight. Immigration officials would have stopped him. Somebody would have stopped him.

"Do you remember what I told you last night? About money buying everything?" Like last night, he looks at me like I'm slow.

"People would have seen."

"Private plane. No one saw, no one who cares."

"You kidnapped me."

"You left me no choice when you a) tried to stab me and b) rammed your knee into my balls."

I look at his neck, at the tiny pinprick of a spot where I broke skin. I was a wimp.

"Next time I'll get it right with the knife," I say.

"If there's a next time, you'll think the way you're feeling right now is a fucking vacation to how you'll be hurting when I'm done with you."

He's not smiling, or smirking, or grinning, or anything.

He's warning me.

And I don't doubt he'll do exactly what he says.

"Where are you taking me?"

"Home. I told you last night. I hope you're not always so forgetful."

"You drugged me, you jerk."

"You left me no choice. I spent a lot of money on you last night."

I scrunch up my forehead, remembering the details.

God, would I have gone through with it if he hadn't been there? Would I have really gone with Madam Liona? Had sex with some stranger?

No. I can't think about that.

"You haven't even thanked me for saving you from whatever pervert had bought your *virginities*. Christ. What a word."

"Why did you do it?"

"Why did I do it?"

I nod.

"Because I'm a selfish man. I want you for myself." Again, he's dead serious, but different. Not threatening violence. Something else.

Something dark but also lonely.

Like there's something empty about him.

I feel a sudden chill and my stomach hurts. Not like I'm going to puke again, though. More like the way I felt after the reaping.

Wanting.

It's the strangest thing. I can't figure it out.

All I know is it's wrong.

The car slows, and I hear the clicking of the turn signal as we take a sharp turn and begin to ride uphill, the road bumpier, unpaved, too narrow to allow for any error in judgment.

Gregory shifts his gaze out the front windshield, and I do the same.

It's winter so the trees are bare. Snow covers the ground and clings to every branch creating an almost postcard-like winter wonderland. The deep orange sunrise has given way to clear blue skies and I know it's utterly still out there. Like you'd hear the flapping of a bird's wings still.

I look at Gregory Scafoni. The stubble along his jaw is thicker.

"How long have I been out?"

He shifts his gaze to me. "Overnight."

We take another turn and he studies me.

I blink, look away.

"I do like your hair like this."

I turn back to him. "Because I look like her?"

I don't know why I ask it. This is part of that strangeness. That wanting. Longing.

His eyes narrow and it's like he's reading me, like he's understanding something.

I return my attention to the snowy scene outside, wipe a hand across my wet eyes hoping he doesn't notice.

There is something seriously wrong with me.

The SUV slows as we approach the rusting, open gates along the ancient stone wall of a huge property.

All around is white, a thick, heavy fall of snow and dense trees, an overgrown garden leading up a winding path to a house I can only see the roof of for a long time. A huge house, an estate, an ancient half-ruin like the stone walls of the perimeter and the tired gate.

And all I can think is how beautiful it is.

How haunting.

Like something time forgot.

Two of the four chimneys smoke, and where snow doesn't cling, I see the terra cotta colored walls associated with all things Italian. There are three floors and on the topmost, the windows are shuttered with wood nailed into the ornate, almost Arabian looking frames.

A large balcony spans the second floor. Snow drapes the huge, twisted branches that weave themselves through the wrought iron railing. There, the wooden shutters stand open, the windows like eyes watching our approach.

And it does feel like that. Like the house is watching us come.

We reach a huge fountain I can almost imagine flowing water in the spring and summer except that it's crumbling. But it's almost more beautiful for the decay.

The driver curves around it to stop in front of the house.

Wide stone steps, three of them, lead up to the porch, which is as wide as the balcony above. It's dry underneath, the snow hasn't penetrated here, and I can see the pretty color of the wall, like that of the sunrise this morning.

There's a fire burning in the large outdoor fireplace and when the door opens, an older woman walks outside wiping her hands on her apron and I smile because for a moment, for a single, fleeting moment, I forget where I am, who I am with, how I got here.

I forget that I am a captive.

A Willow Girl to the beautiful, ruthless Scafoni bastard beside me.

All it takes is the opening of the SUV's door and Gregory's hand like a vice on my arm pulling me across the seat and out of the vehicle to remind me, though. He catches me when I stumble, but he's not looking at me.

His eyes are locked on the house and mine are locked on him.

Home.

He'd said we were going home.

I shiver when an icy gust of wind sends snow up the still-wet legs of my jeans and I hug my arms to myself and Gregory finally turns to me.

"Welcome to Villa de Rossi, Amelia Willow. I hope you'll be very unhappy here."

5

GREGORY

I walk Amelia up toward the front entrance. She isn't struggling but that's probably a combination of feeling weak from the drug and the impossibility of her new situation.

In the beginning when I'd first decided I wanted her, I thought I'd have to make her. And I still do, to some extent, but there's something else too. Some part of her, it's drawn to this.

To the Willow Girl legacy.

To me.

It doesn't mean she won't fight me, though, and it doesn't mean I don't want her to.

She walks ahead of me up the stairs. Her hair will need to be fixed. She must have taken scissors and just cut straight across the back. Chopped off most of it. I'm keeping the dark though. And not because it makes her look like Helena. It doesn't.

They share similarities in features, not coloring, obviously, but the upward turn of their noses, the arrogant set of their cheekbones, the almost doll-like perfect profile. Some mannerisms too, especially the stubborn way they jut out their chins when they don't like something.

Matteo goes to his mother, Irina. He greets her with a kiss on her cheek. It's strange to see him like he is with her. He's twice her size and my right-hand man. I trust him with my life. But with Irina, he's a little kid again.

"Irina," I say.

Matteo steps aside and Irina smiles back to me, saying something in Italian, looking me over, asking if I've been eating well enough. It's been several weeks since I've seen her.

I kiss her cheek and let her hug me. Lucinda, my own mother, never hugged me like this. Irina is more a mother to me than Lucinda ever was.

But Lucinda lacks any warmth. No room left for it with all that hate churning inside her.

"This is Amelia," I tell Irina in Italian.

The older woman smiles warmly, looks her over too, says something about feeding both of us properly.

"Amelia, this is Irina, Matteo's mother." I realize I never actually introduced Matteo.

"Nice to meet you," she says. She rubs her arms for warmth.

"Go inside," I tell her.

She hesitates, glancing back the way we came.

I step toward her, rub her arms, squeeze to make her look at me. "You can freeze out here or go inside where it's warm. Your choice. I don't really care. But those are your only choices."

She mutters something but follows Irina in.

I take a moment to walk the length of the portico, stand before the large stone fireplace to warm my hand—the one that wasn't burnt—as I take in the work done while I've been gone.

The house is more than a century old and has sat empty for most of those years. I'm restoring it to its original grandeur, but I only started the project a year ago even though I've owned it for more. The weather has slowed down construction.

I'm actually the second owner. After the circumstances of the original family leaving Villa De Rossi, the bank couldn't give it away. It's rumored to be haunted by the De Rossi family, both Mother and daughter.

It doesn't bother me, though. Ghosts don't scare me. I've lived with them all my life.

Besides, this is my house now.

My home.

Not theirs.

The house on the island, any of our properties, they've never felt like mine. Or like home. The way Scafoni law is written, although we each inherit a certain sum once we come of age, the first born, or, as is the case now, the oldest living son, is master of the estate of Scafoni.

I snort.

It's a fucking lottery, that.

Besides, he's not technically first born. Timothy is. Was. Hell, maybe Sebastian wrapped that cord around Timothy's neck while they were still in the womb. Maybe he was a fucking killer before he was even born.

I shake it off.

I have my money. None of that matters now.

After what happened on the island, I had an attorney draw up paperwork demanding my share. Demanding I be free of Sebastian. Threatening I'd return to the island to lay claim to his precious Willow Girl because in the end, she isn't marked. She's still fair game.

Hell, maybe that's why I did it, why I grabbed hold of the branding iron. Not to save her at all, but to keep my options open.

Sebastian couldn't wait to be rid of me. Made me sign a counter-agreement that I'd never have contact with Helena again before he agreed to my terms.

I wonder if Helena knows about that.

Or if she's the one who requested it.

There's a nagging thought that what I'm doing now, it's because of her.

Did I take Amelia to hurt Helena?

Or to somehow, in some ridiculous twisting of my warped mind, did I do it to be close to her?

I grit my teeth and pull off the leather glove to make myself remember. I look at the marred skin of my hand. The uneven texture, the crescent so clear.

His mark.

His even though it was me who saved her from the iron. Not him.

And she still chose him.

No. I refuse to go down this road again. I fucking refuse.

Fuck Helena.

Fuck them both.

I hold my hand up to the fire and feel the excruciating pain of it again. Feel the searing of the iron as I closed my hand around it and gripped it tight to me, the pain like nothing I've experienced before or since.

The doctor says I shouldn't feel a thing. That the nerves are dead.

But I feel it.

I feel it like it's happening again right now and as much as I want to pull my hand away, I force myself to keep it in the heat, until it banishes thoughts of her, of that night, of the island, of those months.

Fuck Helena and fuck Sebastian.

This has nothing to do with either of them.

Nothing!

The door opens, and Matteo clears his throat.

I turn my back to him, slide my glove back on.

The sun is high, and a square of snow slides off the roof, landing heavy and loud just a few feet from me. Like it's just been pushed. Like a ghost shoved it to remind me that I'm here. That I can get my head out of my ass now because the past is finished.

Because I have what I always wanted. My own Willow Girl.

I go inside, a tight smile on my face. I'm tired. It's been a long night and I didn't get any sleep.

Amelia is standing in the foyer in front of the man-sized fireplace warming her hands. She's looking at the frescoed ceiling. It's not yet been fully restored, but the original bright colors of the flowers —a garden overhead—is striking. There are more like it throughout the house. Always gardens. Always bright flowers in full bloom.

Strange what's preserved and what decays.

"Some parts of the house are still under construction," I say. "You need take care not to go to those areas."

"How old is it?"

"Over a hundred years."

"Wow."

Irina says something about food. I tell her to give us time to freshen up and take Amelia's backpack.

"Come with me."

She follows me through the large living room

with its matching fireplace, peeks at the dining room table already set for lunch.

"The stairs aren't finished, obviously, so just be careful."

The stone stairs are in pretty good shape, but the banister had rotted and needed replacing so there's just empty space where it should be. The walls are papered in a deep, textured blue. Amelia runs her fingers along it as she follows me up the stairs.

"This place, it's like time forgot it," she says when we reach the second-floor landing.

"People say it's haunted." I walk to the last set of double doors at one end of the hallway.

"Is it?"

I shrug a shoulder, open the doors and gesture for her to enter.

She stops as soon as she does.

The room is beautiful. I designed it myself with four huge leaded glass windows, heavy, ceiling to floor drapes in charcoal and a custom bed at the center with built in nightstands on either side. It's huge and modern and old at once with its wide wooden base. There is a small table and two chairs against the opposite wall but otherwise, the room is bare.

And it's very obviously not a guest room.

I walk in, close the door and set her backpack on the bed.

"Bathroom's through there," I say, pointing. "You should find everything you need."

She walks toward it, notes the book on the nightstand, the jacket hanging over the back of a chair.

The bathroom door closes, and I hear the lock turn and I do a quick mental scan of all the things in there she can try to attack me with. Then I think of searching her and that thought makes me smile.

She comes back into the bedroom ten minutes later looking refreshed. She's washed her face and brushed her teeth. Her hair is pulled into a ponytail.

"Whose room is this?" she finally asks.

"Mine."

"But you have toiletries for me?"

I nod.

"How long were you planning this?"

"A while."

"I'm not sleeping in your bed."

I smile, stalk toward her.

She drops her arms, which were folded across her chest, to her sides. I know it takes all she has to stay where she is and not back up when I'm standing toe to toe with her.

"My bed is exactly where you're sleeping."

"No." But her voice comes out weak.

I put a finger to the middle of her chest, walk her backward to the wall, pin her to it.

She puts her hands to my chest to keep that little bit of distance between us and has to crane her neck to look up at me and all I can think is how small she is. How defenseless.

How mine.

"I won't..." her voice breaks and she has to clear her throat. "I won't sleep with you."

I look her over, the oversized sweater hanging off her shoulder again, lower too, exposing the swell of one breast. I let the knuckles of my hand brush against it, hear her breath catch as her chest heaves. I return my gaze to hers.

"You will. And you'll want it. You'll want it more than you will like to admit."

"Let me go."

"You don't want me to let you go."

She shoves against me. It's kinda cute.

"I see it in your eyes, Amelia. See how your pupils dilate. See how your lips part and your pretty little tongue darts out to lick them. Preparing them for me."

"I'm not...they're not—"

"I even bet if I reach inside your panties..." I let that trail off and slide one hand down over her belly, undo the top button of her jeans.

She clamps both hands over mine, nails digging into skin.

I give her a smile, push my fingers just inside her jeans, just into the waistband of her panties, barely tickling there.

She makes a sound, tries to pull at my wrist.

A full minute passes before I withdraw my hand and step away, releasing her. I draw my sweater over my head, hearing her gasp when I do.

"Are you going to pull any more knives?" I ask.

Her mouth is open. Her eyes glued to my chest. And I imagine it's startling, what she sees.

I go to her, touch her chin with one finger to tilt her face upward.

"Cat got your tongue?"

"You...your..." her eyes slip to the ink covering much of my chest.

"I need a shower and I'm hungry. Are you going to pull any more knives?"

She drags her eyes upward and shakes her head almost absently.

"Why?" she asks. She doesn't mean the knife.

A weight comes over me, like lack of sleep and the trip and the island and the last few months... everything is finally taking its toll. Like now that I'm home, everything will come crashing down around me.

I study her, search her eyes, wanting to see myself through them.

Wanting to see what she sees.

"Because it's the night that changed everything."

6

AMELIA

It's the night that changed everything. Not only for Helena and Sebastian, but for him and me. It's the night that led us here.

I stand there stupidly mute listening to the bathroom door click closed. To the sound of the shower switching on.

He seemed weighed down. Tired. Like when I asked him why, he was just so tired.

I walk across the room to my backpack and take out my notebooks. I sit on the edge of the bed—his bed. Glancing through the sketchbooks, I find the one I'm looking for because I know exactly which one he used. At least for the image I recognized. The ones on his back, I only had a flash of the chaos of ink there.

It will take hours to study his skin.

Days.

I sit looking at the sketch, tracing it with my fingertip, tracing each of the ancient wooden blocks, the smudges of my sisters' faces.

Seeing them, the Scafoni bastards.

The shower switches off, but I barely register it because I'm trying to make sense of what he's done. And when the door opens, I look up at him and he pauses for a second, like he's surprised to see me here. Where would I go?

He has a towel slung low around his hips and his hair is wet and standing up all around his head and all I can do is stare for a long minute. Stare at the past inked on his body, because that's what this is.

"One of my notebooks was missing. I thought I was crazy," I say. I remember looking everywhere. That's when I stopped taking them out of the apartment. Started sketching on bar napkins because I couldn't stop sketching. "Was it you? Did you take it?"

He doesn't answer me, but he doesn't have to. The evidence, it's there. On his chest.

I set the book aside and get up, go to him.

He still has his glove on. Did he shower with it?

But the tattoos draw my attention away from the oddity.

I look more closely, reach up to touch the ink, feel the soft, warm skin stretched tight over hard muscle.

A spark of pure electricity has me snatch my hand back with a gasp.

I look up at him.

He felt it too, I know it. I see it on his face.

I go to walk around him, but he doesn't let me. He turns with me, grinning down at me.

"Let me see," I say.

"It's not for you to see."

"It's what happened. On that island." I know it.

He doesn't answer, but his expression changes, the smile vanishing.

That weight is back.

And I'm locked out.

He walks away, into the large closet. When he returns a minute later, he's wearing a black sweater with dark jeans and is combing his hands through his hair.

"Did you catalogue it?" I ask.

"Don't make a big deal out of it. It's ink. Just ink."

"No. It's more than that. I know it."

"Do you?"

"I want to see."

"I told you, it's not for you to see."

He goes to the door, opens it, gestures for me to go ahead.

"Why?"

"Why what?"

"Why did you do it?"

He doesn't answer me but steps out into the hallway.

"I asked you a question." I follow him.

He stops, half turns like he's bored. But then something else takes over, something darker.

"Ever hear the expression curiosity killed the cat?" he asks, walking me backward until my back is, once again, at the wall.

"I just want to understand."

He brushes the knuckles of his hand down over my cheek, lifting my hair to whisper at my ear: "It'll only make you want it more, Amelia." His voice is deep and his words seductive and taunting at once.

"I don't want it."

He studies me, like he's reading me.

"I see you. I see what's inside you."

"You don't see anything. You don't know me."

"No?"

He sets his big hand on my stomach. It spans almost the whole of it.

I don't move. I barely breathe.

"You know what *I* want, Amelia?" he asks, dipping his head lower so the scruff of his jaw scratches my skin. "I want nothing more than to shove you against this wall, rip off your jeans and fuck that tight virgin pussy of yours. I want to feel you bleed. I want to feel the warmth of virgin blood spill all over my dick."

I make a sound, like a mouse, and his breath at

my ear makes every hair on my body stand on end and his words, his words terrify me and excite me, and he's right. I do want this, in some twisted, freakish way, I want exactly this.

"Did you want to be her? The Willow Girl?" he taunts.

He slides his hand downward, down toward my jeans which are still unbuttoned, and I feel each tooth of the zipper as he drags it down. Feel the slow, deliberate movement of his hand slipping into the waistband of my jeans, my panties.

"Did you want to be the one he chose?" His hand dips lower, fingertips finding the seam of my sex.

"Stop."

"The one he fucked?"

The way he says the word, the almost clicking sound of the *ck*, it's like he can taste it.

He curls his fingers into my folds. It's the first time anyone's fingers but my own have been there. Have touched me there.

And I can't breathe or think or fight.

"Huh? Is that it? You wish he'd chosen you instead of your sister? Dragged you to that island? You wish he'd made *you*?"

I look up at him and all I can feel are his fingers on me and it's hard to think, to breathe, to do anything but look up at him.

He's got a strange look on his face. His eyes appear darker, the turquoise specks bright in contrast and so intent on mine, like he wants to burn his gaze into me, to steal the thoughts from my mind.

"Do you want to be made to, little Willow Girl?"

"No." It's weak and he hears it.

"Because you're wet." This last part, it's a long, drawn out whisper I feel more than hear and I squeeze my eyes shut in shame because he's right.

My hands which should be pushing him away are resting against his chest and when he hooks a finger inside me, I whimper, and I know that's what he wants.

He brings his mouth to mine and he kisses me, but he doesn't dip his tongue inside, not yet, not even when I open to him. Instead, he pulls back, takes my lower lip between his teeth and bites just a little, just enough to cut, to draw a single drop of blood.

I'm clinging to him and he's rubbing my clit and it feels so good and that sound I hear, it's me.

I shouldn't want this.

I shouldn't want him.

But then those caresses turn hard, pain and pleasure alternating, pain dominating as, with his fingers inside me, he draws me up on tiptoe.

"You know what I think?"

I don't say a word. I can't.

"I think you want to be fucked," he says, a hint more anger to his words. More violence.

I swallow, shake my head. But he just twists his fingers inside me.

"Stop," I try.

"I think you're dying to be fucked, in fact."

"You're hurting me."

"Do you like being hurt? Your sister did."

My gaze flies to his. "Stop it!"

"Just one question. Are you dying to be fucked by me or will any Scafoni bastard do?"

I shove at him, finally.

"Stop!"

He doesn't budge but he shifts his grip so he's rubbing my clit again and this time, the sound I make is a moan and it's from deep inside me and I hate him. I do. I hate him.

"Which is it?" he asks.

Is he so unaffected while I unravel before his eyes? While he so easily pulls me apart at the seams?

Because those months in Philadelphia, it's like I knew it was him. Like I've known all along it was him following me. Like a sixth sense.

Like this was always going to happen.

I let my hands slide lower, over sculpted chest and rock-hard abs and then I feel him and he's not unaffected.

No, not unaffected.

I wrap my hand around the steel rod of his cock threatening to tear through his jeans and I lick my lips and he's still rubbing my clit and I'm so close, and when he closes his other hand around the back of my neck and pulls me into him, I drop my head and let my forehead rest against his chest and I'm panting and the sounds I'm making, they're foreign to me.

I should fight him.

I want to want to fight him.

But when I try to pull away, he shifts his grip to my hair and forces me to look at him and he grins.

"Is this what you want?"

I'm pathetic.

I can't even find my fucking voice.

His eyes narrow and he chuckles but there's no joy in the sound. He draws his hand away, brings it to my face, wiping his fingers across my cheek, my mouth, leaving a trail of wetness.

My knees buckle and I'm on the floor and he drops down with me and, with that same hand, pulls my head into his chest.

It's only when my face is buried there that I let go. That I weep. I sob quietly into him, my hands flat against him, shoulders racking, wanting to push him away, knowing I should. Fuck. I should.

But what he said, it's the truth.

He knows it. I know it.

It's wrong.

I'm wrong.

Perverse.

Twisted.

But he's right. And maybe it's shame that has me taking comfort here, against the warm strength of my enemy's chest, my face hidden from him.

My shame hidden from me.

At least momentarily.

He pulls back, stands, and it's like someone's pulled the blanket away it's suddenly so cold.

"Take care you don't fall in love with me, Willow Girl."

I hear his words.

I feel them.

My head is bowed and the stone beneath my knees is smooth and icy and I squeeze my eyes shut like maybe I can disappear. Like maybe if I can't see him then he can't see me.

I think he's going to say something. Humiliate me further. Kick me, maybe. Kick me while I'm down.

But then he moves. He just turns and walks away, walks down the stairs and I watch him go and he doesn't even look back. Not the briefest glance.

Can he even stand to look at me?

7

GREGORY

"She doesn't eat unless she eats with me."

"I can take a sandwich up—" Irina starts, already holding a plate in her hands.

I look up from my desk. It's been hours since that episode. Amelia hasn't been down and Irina, a typical Italian mother, wants to feed her. And as much as I appreciate her concern, she'll do as I say in my house.

I won't make the mistake my brother did.

I won't coddle my Willow Girl.

Matteo walks up behind her. He gets one look at me, takes her gently, shakes his head no as he leads her away.

I get up, pick up the bottle of whiskey. It's early but fuck that. I haven't slept in twenty-four hours and I'm fucking tired.

Not bothering with a glass, I take the bottle and

walk out into the corridor, around the corner and down the hallway to the library, to where the house is darker, still waiting to be updated. It's colder here too, but it's because everything is still shut off here. No heat.

In the library, I pick my way over the rubble using the colored light that's filtering in from the stained-glass window. Snow circles overhead and I look up to see the hole in the glass. I don't think it was there the last time I was here but maybe it was, and I wasn't paying attention.

I stand for a minute watching that white, powder swirl, like dust, as the wind blows it in.

This room, it's strange. I don't waste my time thinking about ghosts. I don't give a fuck if the house is haunted. But I admit, the feeling in this particular room, it's different.

I take a drink from my bottle and step over construction materials and dust and make my way to the back of the deceptively large room to a door that looks older than the house itself. A solid heavy, dark wooden door.

I take out my key, it's an old fashioned one but that too I don't want to change. I unlock it, push it open, take out my phone to light the way. No electricity down here.

There's an immediate drop in temperature, a dampness that smells like rot, like the room under the mausoleum on the island.

I take comfort in it.

It makes sense, I guess. For someone as cold as me, as rotten on the inside, a place like this, it's home.

I follow the stone steps down into the catacombs. According to the maps, they go on for miles. Supposedly you can access the village through them, but I haven't yet explored them that closely.

There's just one room I like to go to.

I shine the light down the dark tunnel. Water drips somewhere in the distance, the sound echoing off the walls. Something scurries away as I take a step, looking into the rooms I pass, empty caves, really, this one used to store wine, that one food, the other I don't know. All unused now. Unusable.

The corridor splits into two here. I turn right, and at the next split, another right. It's like a maze.

At the very end of this tunnel is the room I seek. It's the only one with a door. I peer in through the small, barred window and push it open, careful to push the door stop into its hole in the ground so it doesn't close. There's no way to open the door from the inside. Makes me wonder what they used it for.

From my pocket I retrieve my lighter and light the candles along the jutting stones of the walls that I use as shelves. I switch off the flashlight on my phone and put it away. After walking around the room to light every candle, I sit down on the edge of the cot.

It was me who took her sketchbook. It was one of her first.

And here they are, all those drawings, black and white, the corners curling from the humidity down here, some too wet from the wall they're stuck to. I sit, and I drink my whiskey and look at them, that night sketched from every angle.

Funny how some minds work.

These sketches, they're like peering into her head. A glimpse where I'm not allowed.

It's how she saw that night, the night of the reaping. How she saw the scene that she was forced to be a part of, that lasted mere minutes and that changed everything.

And me looking at these drawings, it feels like I'm spying.

She memorized all the details. Even our faces. Although those aren't quite right. Ethan is a blur. Sebastian looks like Satan. Me, I look like myself, sort of, but she's missing something.

I swallow a little more of the whiskey, get up. Go to one of the sketches and take the stub of charcoal from the shelf below. I fix the details of our faces. Add shadow to the corners of the library. Because that's where the ghosts of the dead Willow Girls lurked in their house.

Her focus that night, it would have been on my brother.

On him and Helena.

I'm surprised at the detail of my face.

I look at the sketch where Sebastian's lifted Helena's shift. I added color to that one. It's one of only two with color in any of these sketches. A smear of red. The marking. I wonder if it was that that drew my brother.

But I would have chosen Helena too then. She was the one who stood out.

Maybe her parents did that on purpose. Binding her like they did. Gagging her. Maybe it was to safeguard their golden daughters and give up the one they loved least.

No.

I don't know if they loved her less than the others.

I don't know if they loved any of them at all. Because if they did, how could they have put them on those blocks?

I sit back down smudging charcoal on the label of the whiskey bottle as I pick it up. The liquid burns its way down my throat. I rub my eyes. I'm tired. I should sleep.

What happened up there, at the end, I didn't expect that. That quiet, desperate sobbing.

And even though I think I understand her, at least in some way, that part confused me.

I know what I said is right. Hell, she confirmed it with just the look on her face. With the reaction of her body.

I bring my fingers to my nose. The faintest scent of her lingers and I inhale deeply, finding it hard to swallow.

She's different than I thought she would be.

In the time I've been watching her, she's been different than what I expected.

I figured it was her dealing with the knowledge that her parents betrayed her. Betrayed all of the sisters, really. Her mother, who'd survived a reaping herself, who'd witnessed what the Willow Girl legacy did to her own sister, still put her daughters on those blocks.

I can see how that would fuck with you.

But when I went into her apartment and found those sketches, I saw something different. Felt it.

Longing.

It's what I can't get out of my head.

It's what I feel when I see these sketches.

It's what draws me to her.

Binds me to her.

And that sobbing. Her leaning into me. Almost taking shelter in me.

Me.

I drink a long swallow of whiskey, study the pictures that surround me, and all I can think is that she's fucked up.

As fucked up as me.

8

AMELIA

When I wake up, it's to that orange glow coming in from the windows. I never closed the curtains.

I look to the other side of the bed, but it's empty. And it hasn't been slept in. The bathroom door is open, and the light is out. Same with the closet. I'm alone.

After he left me on the stairs, I locked myself in the bathroom for a while. I thought he'd come back. Honestly, I wasn't sure if I wanted him to or not.

I took a shower, put my same clothes back on because the only thing I have in my backpack are those sketch books. I don't think he brought the duffel bag. But I guess he had his hands full with me and my backpack after he knocked me out.

My headache has dulled although it's not gone completely and I'm so hungry, my stomach hurts. I get up, feeling sticky. Sleeping in a sweater and jeans wasn't the smartest thing but the alternative was my underwear and since I'm sleeping in his bed, I'm not doing that.

I go to the window, watch the sunrise. It's beautiful. I never really took time to watch it before. It must be freezing out because snow still coats every branch and where the rising sun hits, ice crystals sparkle like diamonds.

In the bathroom, I wash my face, brush my teeth and hair. My reflection still surprises me, the dark so different to the blonde I'm used to. If I'd had more time, I'd have gone to a hairdresser and done it properly. Well, if I had time and money. The latter is how I got into this mess with Charlie and Madam Liona.

I'd met Charlie a few days after arriving in Philadelphia. He'd introduced himself to me and handed me a business card for his modeling agency. He'd told me I had the look they were searching for and like the dummy I am, I fell for it hook, line and sinker.

I never did have any modeling jobs, but Charlie told me he'd set me up in the apartment. That it belonged to a friend and that I could pay her back when I got paid. He bought me clothes. A phone. Gave me some cash.

Talk about the perfect scam.

Not to mention the perfect fool.

It's cliché, really. A young, naïve girl from the

Midwest gets to the big city on her own and immediately falls victim to a con man.

But did Gregory save me or did I jump out of the frying pan and into the fire?

I think about what he said. Did I want to be the Willow Girl? Did I want Sebastian to have chosen me?

These are the questions I've been avoiding outright asking myself for months. And he saw it in a matter of hours. He read me like a book.

When I return to the bedroom, I hear a quiet knock on the door. I know instantly it's not Gregory because I am sure he would never knock and if he did, it wouldn't be so soft.

I go to it, open it.

The woman I met yesterday is standing outside. She's holding a tray with coffee and slices of steaming bread with butter, jam and a plate of cheeses.

"You haven't eaten," she says with a warm, concerned smile. Her accent is pretty.

My mouth waters at the scent of coffee and freshly baked bread.

I look beyond her, almost expecting him.

"He's gone," she says. She gestures as if asking if she can come inside.

I move aside. "Thank you," I say, and I feel like I want to cry at this kindness.

She sets the tray down on a table in the corner.

"Do you know where he is?"

She shakes her head.

"Or when he'll be back?" God, I sound pathetic.

"No."

She leaves and closes the door and I pour myself a cup of coffee with a generous serving of cream. The first sip is heaven and I sit down to butter the bread and I eat every bite.

When I've emptied the carafe of coffee and only crumbs remain of the food, I get up, take the tray, steel my spine and walk out the door.

First thing I do is find the kitchen to return the tray. The woman takes it from me, and I thank her again before going inside. I'm cautious at first, but pretty soon, I know he's not lurking around some corner somewhere, waiting to pounce.

I spend the morning looking into various rooms of the house, peering down hallways that are under construction. No one is working on the house today. I guess the weather is keeping them all away.

The second floor is the closest to being finished with only two rooms still sealed off. I take the stairs to the third floor, taking care as some of the stone has crumbled. But when I reach the landing, it's almost pitch-black and each of the three doors are boarded up.

And, quite frankly, it's creepy up here, so I make my way back downstairs.

On the main floor are the grand foyer, the living

and dining rooms, kitchen, a locked room and a library.

The library is in the middle of construction and it's chilly in here. The windows must be original. They're stained glass and as beautiful as they are, they do nothing to keep the cold out.

I hug my arms to myself and make my way around the room. The style in here is more gothic than the rest of the house, darker and seeming older. I wonder if he'll try to keep it looking like this.

There's an ancient looking armchair that's so worn, there's a rip in the faded leather of the seat. I touch a spot where the brass buttons are missing as I make my way around some of the construction materials to get to the bookshelves.

I scan the books. They're dusty, like they were left here ages ago. I wonder about the history of the house.

A flutter draws my attention and I look up at the ceiling. This one, like the one in the foyer, is frescoed. Beautiful flowers create a sort of garden in shades of sky-blue, green, magenta and yellow. It's so pretty, I turn a circle to look at it when I see the flutter again.

It makes me jump because it's a bird. It must have gotten trapped inside while the workers were here.

It flies across the ceiling again. I recognize the type of bird. A robin. It makes me smile because I see robins everywhere I go. But this one, she's obviously in distress. I wonder how long she's been locked up in here.

I inspect the windows more closely and try to pull on the lever to open it, but it's either stuck or sealed so I stop. Looking up higher, there's a break in the glass big enough for the bird to have flown through. Which explains the puddle of water on the floor where the wind blows snow in.

The armchair is too heavy to move, but I see an old table covered in inches of dust in the far corner. Picking my way around the debris on the floor, I get to it, distracted by the shelves of books, like a maze, the room bigger than it appeared when I first entered.

I sneeze when I clear off the dust and test that it's sturdy enough to take my weight before carrying it to the window. It's low enough for me to climb on and if I stand on it, I should be able to reach the hole in the window, but I'll have to catch the bird first.

She's perched on a high shelf watching me. I'll need to coax her down.

Taking care to close the door quietly behind me, I head back into the hallway and to the warmer part of the house. Irina is cooking something and smiles at me, watches me slice off a piece of the same bread I ate earlier. She doesn't ask any questions as I take a bite of it and walk back out.

I return to the library and the bird is still in the

same place. I whistle softly and make crumbs of the bread, setting most of them on a shelf and stepping away. When I'm far enough, the bird flies down and starts to pick at the food. Poor thing must have been starving.

As quietly as I can, I approach her and I'm sure she's going to fly away, but she doesn't. Instead, she stops eating and looks at me for a moment before returning her attention to the crumbs.

I reach out, my palms open. She sees the crumbs in my hand and hops on to peck at them, her little beak sharp, like a pin prick. When I close my other hand around her back, she chirps, flaps her wings.

"Shh. It's okay," I tell her as I carry her to the window.

Getting on the table is harder without being able to hold on to something but I manage it and a moment later, I push my hands through the broken glass and set the bird free. The last of the bread crumbs fall from my hand as I watch it go. When I go to pull my hands in, I'm not as careful and wince as the sharp glass cuts the back of my hand.

Blood slides over my skin, a deep, dark red. It doesn't hurt, but I stand there momentarily mesmerized, holding my arm up, watching it trail over my thumb and to my wrist. Only when it drops to the floor do I wipe it away and climb back down.

I find a roll of paper towels probably left by the construction crew and hold a sheet over my hand as

I return to the back of the library, to the maze of shelves, running my fingers over the spines of the books, looking at the binding, mostly leather, taking a few out and reading the publication dates, late 1800s or very early 1900s.

I wonder if he'll keep the books. I hope he will. Maybe he'll let me clean them, dust them off, organize them. Some are too old and in too poor shape to be salvaged but many are fine.

Most of the shelves are neat, even for the dust, but when I get to the end of one, there's a stack of folders and notebooks. I pick through the stack and find the original plans of the house, looking at notes in the margins, unable to understand most as they're in Italian.

In one of the notebooks, someone's sketched various rooms, interiors and exteriors, even the gardens. It's fascinating, and when I get to the two faded photographs of the house and the family posed in front of it, my curiosity gets the better of me.

It's a couple and their little girl, the man and woman smiling, their daughter beaming. The mom has her hands on her little girl's shoulders, and it looks like she's about to run after her puppy who is a blur.

I walk it to the window for better light and wipe it clean of dust and peer more closely at their faces. The man is bearded and looks to be in his forties. He has dark hair and is wearing a formal wool suit. From the foliage, it must be fall.

His wife—I assume it's his wife—is beautiful. She looks quite a bit younger than him and is dressed in a flowing white dress, not as stiff as his suit. Her hair is blonde and her eyes light. The little girl is an exact replica of her mother.

It's only when I look closer that I see the man has his hands on his wife's shoulders and that one of them, it appears to almost be wrapped around the back of her neck, like he's holding on to her, like he's afraid she'll run away if he releases her, just like their daughter who is about to sprint after her little puppy.

I also notice that they're gloved, his hands.

I look more closely at their smiles after noticing this detail and see the tension in his, like it's forced. Like he doesn't belong there with them, the woman and the girl too light, too bright because there's a darkness to him.

A sudden chill makes me shudder and I rub my arms. I return the photograph to its folder but take it and the notebooks to the armchair.

I sit down, slipping off my shoes and tucking my feet underneath me and set them on my lap to begin going through them. The one that captures my attention is from an English paper, the article cut out, the headline sensational.

Count Leonardo de Rossi Cleared of Murder!

Late Saturday night, police released Count Leonardo de Rossi and took him home to Villa de Rossi after weeks of questioning.

When asked to comment, the count's attorney said it was a terrible crime to hold a man who is clearly grieving for the loss of his family in a prison cell and made sure to point out there was no evidence to link the count to the gruesome murder of his wife and the disappearance of their beautiful daughter.

The detective in charge of the investigation has been removed from the case.

There were few clues at the scene the count discovered upon returning from a weekend abroad to find his wife dead, her face badly disfigured, a crime of passion.

According to the coroner, she'd been dead for hours when he discovered her on Christmas morning.

Even more eerie is the disappearance of the little girl. Only four years old, one of her shoes was found at the entrance of the catacombs, but a thorough search has led to nothing.

Any hope to find the killer is growing dim as police have exhausted every lead.

The article ends abruptly.

It happened on Christmas. He found her on Christmas morning. The timing makes it even more terrible.

I don't recognize the name of the publication, but this is so old, they're probably out of business. Is it a gossip magazine or a reputable paper? Because there's no doubt the assumption is that the count killed his wife and maybe his daughter?

I leaf through more clippings and come across another one dated almost one year after that article was published. It's torn but from what I can make out, the newspaper was marking the one-year anniversary of the gruesome crime and the fact that it has never been solved. They also state that the count abandoned the house, a home he'd built for his family, and returned to San Gimignano, the city of his birth.

One more clipping from six years later shows the house in terrible condition with a note that it is for sale.

From the bits and pieces I can make out from the Italian clippings, the count's wife's first name was Margot and his daughter was named Belle.

I am more curious than ever.

I rub my eyes and glance to the window to see the sky growing dark. It's late afternoon.

Sorting the sheets of paper, I replace most of them on their shelf but take the sketchbook of which the second half is still empty and tuck the photograph inside along with the two newspaper articles in English. I check the hallway before slipping out of the library.

Still no sign of Gregory. I don't know if that's a good thing or a bad thing.

I'm hungry so I head into the kitchen, Irina points out the table set for one and I sit down. I sip the wine and eat the meal she's prepared, a homemade pasta with red sauce and a salad.

"Do you know where Gregory is?" I ask.

She gets a worried expression on her face and says something I don't understand but the shake of her head tells me that's a no.

I don't know why I ask. I'm not unhappy that he's not here, but I'm also trapped in this house without even a proper pair of boots to go outside or even a change of clothes.

After I eat, I wander around the house, looking for a TV or something to keep me from boredom. I should have grabbed a book from the library but it's too dark in there now, at least that's what I tell myself when I get to the door because that icy cold makes me shudder and I turn back to the living room where Irina stacks logs on the fire before slipping away.

There, I find a bottle of whiskey and pour myself some even though I don't really drink the stuff or at least never have before.

I sit in one of the two armchairs and watch the fire, taking off my shoes and tucking my knees up under me, enjoying the warmth and crackle of damp logs.

After drinking some of the whiskey, I rest my head on the arm of the chair and let my eyes close, just for a few minutes. It's warm here with the fire and I don't want to be in his bed. I know I should get up. I should stay alert. But I'm tired and it's dark and quiet and I can't resist the pull of sleep.

I know I'm dreaming when I see the little girl from the photographs running through the house, this house. I know it's her. I have no doubt. She's laughing and chasing her puppy. Everything is as it was then, the house beautiful and light and bright. And warm. So warm, I can almost smell bread baking in the kitchen and feel her laughter as much as hear it.

I'm in awe of it all and following her down corridor after corridor, but looking all around me, not really watching where I'm going. Just knowing I'm following her.

But that light, that warmth, it changes. And it's not a gradual change.

With a shudder I slow just as she does as she runs toward the hall leading to the library.

I don't want to go there and I don't want her to go there.

I try to reach out for her, to stop her. I know it's a dream, but I still want to stop her.

It grows colder as we near that room, me following her toward it and it's urgent now, the need to stop her from going in there.

But when she glances back at me, her face, it's different. Corpse-like, at least momentarily.

Like there's a flash of skull just for a single bone-chilling moment, so quick that when I blink it's gone and she's the pretty little girl again. But she's no longer laughing. Not even smiling. And I stop chasing her because she's stopped running. Like she, too, knows what she'll find inside.

She opens the library door. I hear it creak and hug my arms against the cold.

"Don't," I say.

But she's not listening to me. I don't even know if she hears me.

"Mama," she calls out as she enters, and her voice is sweet and searching, and she's so young. Too young for what she'll find.

It's blood I see first.

The little girl's pretty, white satin ballet slippers soaking it up when she steps to the edge of that widening circle of blood.

She doesn't scream right away. She just looks down and cocks her head to the side like she doesn't understand what she sees.

I don't want to look but I do.

And I see the once beautiful woman lying there, faceless, holes where here pretty eyes were, bone showing through torn skin and blood. So much blood.

Her dead mother.

The little girl's puppy mewls by her side.

She's crying, the little girl, and so am I.

I want to tell her to turn away, to come to me. But it's too late and she steps into the pool of blood and her little shoe leaves the smallest print.

The puppy is barking now.

I follow the little girl's gaze as the puppy disappears behind a bookshelf.

"Don't go," I try to tell her, but my voice makes almost no sound and I find myself following her, reaching out to catch her as she steps over her mother's corpse.

My hand slips through her ghost-like form as she chases after her puppy and I try not to look down as I, too, step over the woman's lifeless body.

I'm barefoot and the blood is dark and almost sticky when it drips thick and warm off my foot and I can't look away, not until I hear the girl again. Hear her say something and her voice sounds different. Scared. And I think she's calling for help.

"I'm coming," I say.

A door creaks open and I drag my gaze from the blood and follow, leaving red footprints on the dusty floor.

It seems like I'm running for hours, days, in this never-ending maze until I reach the end. I see her face again, that of the child again, like she's been waiting for me. When she sees me, she reaches her hand out, and when I reach mine to hers, she giggles like it was all just a game, and pulls away and disappears down into a darker space, and I hear her giggles echo and look at her ruined shoe, the white satin a dirty red, left behind as she disappears until there's almost no sound at all, not until I hear my name.

"Amelia."

It's a man's voice. I look around but there's no one here.

I try to take another step toward where the little girl disappeared, but I can't seem to move. I try again, but I'm caught on something.

"Amelia."

I struggle, but whatever or whoever has got me won't let me go.

That giggle comes, so faint. So sad. And maybe it's not a giggle but a cry.

"I'm coming." My voice sounds strange, like the words aren't fully formed.

"Amelia," he says, his voice firmer, hands rougher.

I open my eyes.

No.

My eyes were open.

I just couldn't see.

He's shaking me.

"I have to go," I say. I don't know why he won't let me go.

Gregory's forehead is furrowed and he's watching me. "Go where?"

I blink. Look around.

"What the hell was that?" he asks.

I'm in the living room, heading toward the hallway in my dream. Heading toward the library.

"Hey." He gives me another shake. "Can you hear me?"

I look back at him. Shrug off his hands. "Of course, I can hear you." I run a hand through my hair, wipe away the beads of sweat on my forehead.

This hasn't happened in years.

Not since I was little. And then once more. On my sixteenth birthday.

Helena woke me that time.

I'd go to the library at home. Always the library. Because libraries are haunted places.

"What just happened?" he asks.

I step backward, my foot sticky, wet on the tiles and for a moment, I think I'm going to see red when I look down. But then I realize what the warmth of blood was. The undrunk whiskey in my glass, I must have turned the cup over, spilled it and stepped into it.

The glass is lying on its side on the floor. I look down at it. It's not broken at least.

The fire flares then dims in the fireplace and I turn to it. It's almost out. I should put another log in it.

"Amelia?" Gregory asks. "Your eyes were open, but I don't think you could see me."

I bend down, right the glass then straighten. I'm trembling.

"It's nothing."

It's dark in here. The fire was the only source of light.

He's still watching me curiously when I look up at him.

"Didn't look like nothing," he says.

"Just a bad dream."

"Were you sleepwalking?"

"No," I lie. "I was going to put wood into the fire."

It's so quiet here, so eerily quiet and I glance at the opening at the far end of the room that leads to the library and it looks like a mouth.

We had ghosts in our library too, I remind myself. I asked my sisters about them once. Asked who they were. I still remember how they looked at me. We were maybe eight at the time and I'd been seeing glimpses of them all my life. I thought everyone saw them.

But after that time, I never asked again.

And our ghosts, they were different than this little girl and her mother. They hadn't been murdered.

The image of the mother's destroyed face flashes in my memory and I shudder. I kneel down, very aware of Gregory's eyes on me, and pick up two logs, push them into the fireplace. With a poker, I try to restart the fire but can't seem to get it going.

"Just a bad dream," he repeats my words, crouching down, taking the poker from me, pushing at the logs, restarting the fire without trouble.

I watch the flames, then turn to him to see the eerie shadows the fire casts across his face.

He stands, fills a glass with whiskey and sips it, still studying me.

"How long have you been here?" I ask.

He refills the glass I spilled and sets it on the table between the armchairs, sitting on one and gesturing for me to sit on the other.

"Not long. You were talking," he says casually. "You said you had to go. Where did you have to go?"

I feel embarrassed and suddenly cold as if a wind has just blown in.

"I don't remember," I lie again. "What time is it?"

"Two o'clock."

"Two in the morning?"

He nods.

I've been out for hours.

"You're not going to tell me?" he asks.

I study his eyes, darker in this dark room. I shake my head once.

He looks me over, pauses at my feet, seems to accept it.

"I ordered some clothes for you. They'll be here in the morning."

I just nod.

"Sit." He points to the second armchair.

"I'm cold."

He pushes the glass toward me. I notice how his fingertips are blackened, appearing dirty.

"Sit with me."

His request—the way he words it—sounds strange.

I go, sit down on the armchair beside his.

He smells like damp and earth.

He gestures to the second glass of whiskey and I take it. I drink a sip and the burning, it's somewhat calming. Warming.

"Tell me about the dream at least."

"I saw the little girl," I say, staring into the fire, drinking more of the whiskey. "And her mother." I turn to him. "Her dead mother."

"I didn't know you were prone to sleepwalking."

"I'm not prone to sleepwalking."

"I know what I saw." He gestures to the things I'd brought out of the library. "You need to stay out of the rooms that are still under construction. The house is very old. You can get hurt.

"And you care if I get hurt?"

He shrugs a shoulder.

"Or is it that you want to do the hurting?"

"Just stay out of those rooms," he says, drinking his whiskey. "They'll give you bad dreams," he adds with a smirk.

"Did you know the story when you bought it?"

He nods, studying me.

"Did he do it? The count?"

"That would be my guess."

"It's colder there. I thought it was just the window, but…"

"The heating's turned off in there. That's all." He swallows the last of his whiskey and I'm not sure he believes what he just said.

"It's different than that."

"Ghosts can't hurt you, Amelia. It's the living you have to watch out for."

9

GREGORY

She studies me just like I did her while she slept. While she dreamt.

"What you said," she starts, pausing, looking at the fire for a long moment before turning back to me. "About me wanting it. Wanting to be the Willow Girl, it's not true."

"No?"

She shakes her head. "But after that night...after Helena was gone, I couldn't stop thinking about it. About the ceremony. My parents refused to talk about it. My sisters, they're more obedient. I'm in between them and Helena, I guess."

"She was the black sheep of the family?"

"I don't know. Our parents were different with her. Always a little harder on her. I thought it was because she was the oldest of us."

"By a few minutes."

"I'm not making an excuse for them. It was easier being me, I know. And Helena always defended us, protected us. And in thanks, we just let your brother take her. Didn't even put up a fight."

I pour more whiskey and turn to the fire. "Don't worry about Helena. She's fine. More than fine."

"I'm happy for her that she is. You're not, though."

I feel her eyes burning a hole in the side of my head.

"Why not? Why aren't you happy for her? For your brother?"

I swallow the whiskey in my glass. It tastes bitter. I turn to her.

"Tell me what you did after that night."

I wonder how much Helena told her about what happened on the island. She doesn't know about me, my part in our doomed ménage-a-trois. I wonder if I told her if it would bring her estimation of her sister down a notch or two or a hundred.

Wonder what it would do to her estimation of me.

"I kept going back into the library. Every night for weeks, I couldn't sleep, and I just kept going back in there. I knew where they'd stored the blocks." She looks down at the glass in her hands. "Funny that all my life I saw them in a corner, just stacked up, not really hidden. I never knew what they were or what they would be used for and it never occurred to me to ask."

She drinks a sip, is silent, but I know she's not finished yet.

"I stood on one again," she says. "I don't know why."

She turns to the fire and I watch the shadow of the flames dance on her face.

"I looked for the sheaths too, the horrible, stinking things we were made to wear. I think if I'd found those, I would have put one on." She chances a glance at me. "That's what I did after that night."

"Did it help?"

"No. I think it did the opposite. I couldn't let it go." There's a long pause. "And I don't know. I mean, I don't *think* I wanted to be chosen. But I didn't want my sisters to be taken from me either."

Her straightforward honesty surprises me. I never expected her to answer my questions.

"And in a weird way, I knew he'd choose Helena anyway," she continues.

I did too. If I think about it.

But I don't say it out loud.

"I was there when she called you," I tell her.

She doesn't seem surprised by this.

"Is that why you chose me? Not my sisters? Because Helena chose to call me?"

I swirl the last sip of whiskey in my glass, swallow it, look at her. "Yes."

She doesn't react when I say it, as if she knew my answer, and the silence grows heavy.

"You chose me to punish her?"

I drink. I don't answer.

"Were you in love with her?"

She looks right at me, her eyes bright and the question, it comes out of nowhere and I am wholly unprepared.

"Is that why I'm here? In order to hurt her?"

I set my glass down, study the intricate pattern of the crystal. "Careful, Amelia."

"Is it? I'm being honest with you. The least you can do is be honest with me. You owe me that, I think. After everything."

"I owe you nothing," I say, looking back at the fire, still somewhat calm. "Go to bed."

"I'm not tired."

"It'll be better for you if you do as I say and go to bed. Now."

"You didn't bring me all the way here just to send me to bed."

I slowly turn to her, watch her swallow a sip of whiskey as a log crackles and spits. She's testing.

She reaches across the table between our chairs, tentatively touches my gloved hand. "Why do you wear this?"

I watch her fingers caress the leather.

"What are you hiding?" she continues.

I don't move when she reaches my wrist, teases the glove down a little.

"Helena said—"

In an instant, I flip my hand over and capture her wrist.

She gasps as I yank her from her chair and to her knees before me. Panic fills her pretty blue eyes when I pull her closer and lean in so I'm inches from her face.

"Don't play games with me."

"Did I hit a nerve?" she asks.

She grits her teeth when I grip a handful of hair and tug her head backward, her free hand clasping my forearm.

"Did I?" she asks again, her voice different because of the angle of her head.

"I'm going to tell you just once more to be careful."

"I'm not scared of you."

"No?" I drag her to kneel up. "You sure about that?"

No answer.

I grin, cock my head to the side. Releasing her wrist, I grip the collar of her sweater and, in one quick tug, rip it down the middle.

She lets out a small, surprised scream and I look at her, that pretty red bra cupping her small breasts, lifting them, making them swell so invitingly.

"Still not scared?" I ask, reaching into one of

those cups, lifting her breast out, feeling the nipple harden against my thumb. Meeting her eyes, I drag her to stand, pull her to me, take her nipple into my mouth and suck hard.

Her hands close over my shoulders as she tries to steady herself, and when she sets one knee on the chair, I capture it between my thighs. I watch her eyes as I close my teeth around her nipple and draw it out.

She lets out a whimper, a sound between pain and pleasure. A flush creeps along her neck, and her eyes darken.

I push her back to her knees, leaving one breast exposed, the flesh around her nipple red from the abuse of my mouth. I lean in toward her.

"So, you don't want this?" I taunt, undoing my belt, opening it, unbuttoning to top button of my jeans.

Her breath is shallow, and her eyes dart from my eyes to my lap and back.

I let go of her hair and she falls backward, massages her scalp. I slide to my knees on the floor and we're so close that our thighs are touching.

"You don't want it?" I ask, undoing her jeans, watching her face as I tug them down.

With one hand on the middle of her chest, I push her backward so she's lying on her back.

"Then fight me," I say, kneeling over her, gripping her panties and taking them down too.

She plants one foot on the floor, tries to push away, but I catch her.

"Come on," I say, letting my gaze fall to her shaved pussy, to the glistening seam of her sex. "You can do better than that."

I dip my head down, and when her hands fist my hair, I grip her wrists and draw them apart as I taste her, lick the wetness from her, listen to her gasp when I take her clit into my mouth and suck.

"Stop!" she commands, her voice high and desperate.

I don't. I suck a little harder, hearing her breath hitch, hearing her whimper, her resistance weak. Only when she pushes her pussy into my face do I pull away, releasing her wrists, looking down at her as she lies wholly exposed to me.

"Fight me," I say, wiping the back of my hand across my mouth. I grip her jeans and panties with one hand to drag them off her legs.

That animates her, but when she sits up, she only manages to help my cause because I pull her jeans off so she's naked from the waist down. Her sweater hangs off one shoulder and she looks fierce as she shoves it off the other and she's up on her knees and lurching for me, hands like claws going for my face, my neck.

I laugh, capture her wrists, drag them to her sides, then behind her, transferring them to one hand.

When I lean in to kiss her, her teeth snap together to bite, making me laugh again.

"That's it," I say, dragging my sweater over my head with my free hand. She's instantly distracted by the ink, trying to make sense of the scene. "That's the fight I'm looking for."

I get to my feet, draw her up to stand with me.

She's fighting, twisting and turning to free herself. She isn't expecting me to release her so when I do, she stumbles backward, dangerously close to the fire.

I catch her arm, steady her.

She pulls away and I look down at her standing there naked but for her bra. I pull her to me, her skin warm against my bare chest, her hair soft under my chin. I reach behind her to unhook her bra, relieve her of it.

"Stop!"

With a handful of hair in my hand, I keep her steady and I kiss her, knowing she'll bite, expecting the sting of skin breaking, tasting the metallic taste of my own blood.

I pull her head into my neck, rub my jaw against the side of her face.

"It makes me hard when you fight," I whisper.

I abruptly release her.

Again, she stumbles backward, but this time, she catches herself.

"You're crazy!" she screams, wiping the back of

her hand across her lip, looking at the smear of my blood on her skin.

I step toward her and she backs into the stone wall of the fireplace.

"Now run, Willow Girl. Run. And don't let me catch you."

When I step back, she's confused. It takes her a full minute and me fake lunging toward her for her to run, and she turns in the direction of the front door. I take my time stalking toward her because there's nowhere she can go that I won't catch her.

When I reach her, she's trying the door, but it's locked tight.

"Run, Willow Girl."

She does, running back into the house, pausing at the stairs, changing her mind and coming back through the living room and toward the dark corridor that leads to the library. She stops at the study door, tries it, but it, too, is locked.

I follow and when she realizes the only escape is into the library, she hesitates, glances back over her shoulder at me, watches me coming for her.

"It's what you want, isn't it?" I ask calmly as I near. "Me chasing you? Me making you?"

She opens the library door and, again, stops. It's dark inside, the moonlight filtered by the stained-glass windows that break letting in the purest silver light, just enough to see.

When she's inside, she turns to close the heavy

door. I wonder if she knows there's no lock. But I don't give her a chance to find out. I set my foot between the door and the frame and she jumps back when I give her a wide smile, pushing it open.

She's walking backwards and trips over something on the floor.

I catch her before she falls, taking her by the arms and pulling her soft, warm body to me, walking her back to the wall.

"Stop! Let me go!"

"You don't want me to let you go."

She's shoving at my chest, but I press mine against her and trap her to the wall as I reach to undo my jeans, push them down a little, just enough.

She makes a panicked sound, a whine, and her face contorts.

"Please."

"Still not scared of me?" I ask, lifting one leg, hoisting her up a little.

Her hands close over my shoulders. She swallows, and I feel her heart drum against my chest and a tear slides down her cheek.

"I'm scared," she whispers, and I think she's scared of a thousand things.

My cock is at her entrance and she feels warm and wet and her nipples press like pebbles against my chest. And when another tear falls, I watch it and she's not pushing me away and she's not fighting or digging her nails into me or trying to get away from me.

"I'm scared," she repeats.

"Strange Willow Girl." I touch her cheek, trace a tear and I mean what I say. She is strange. Different. And in a way, I understand her. "To want this. Like this."

She doesn't answer. Doesn't say yes or no or anything. Just watches me as more tears slide down her cheeks.

I move a little, feeling the tightness of her pussy against the head of my cock.

Her fingernails dig into my shoulders.

"If you want me to stop, then say it. Now."

She doesn't.

"Say it, Amelia."

Nothing. Nothing as her sad blue eyes search mine.

"Say it."

"I don't..."

"Weak."

"I don't want it."

"Weaker yet."

"I don't want *you*!"

Something dark takes hold of me.

She studies me for a long moment but then she lowers her gaze, drops her head, pulls herself into me, clinging to me, her actions wholly opposite of her words. And I know what she's saying, it isn't true.

But she is weak.

She can't own what she wants.

I force her head up, her face small in my hand, her tears wet beneath my fingers pressing into her cheeks.

"Then tell me to stop."

She looks away, just beyond me.

"Tell me to stop."

Nothing.

"I'm right, aren't I?" I ask, finally.

She tries to break free, but I press the back of her head against the wall and make her look at me. Because she needs to look at me when I do this.

She needs to see me for who I am. What I am.

To know in spite of everything, that she still wants it. Wants me.

"I'm right. You want this—me—like this, more than you're willing to admit. And that's what makes you weak. Not the wanting."

I push into her and I'm not gentle.

And when I feel her barrier, I thrust hard.

Her nails break the skin of my back as the warm gush of her virgin blood saturates my cock and fuck she's tight and wet and so fucking warm and she's clinging to me. Clinging, not fighting. Not pushing me away.

I let go of her face and she dips her head into the crook of my neck, and I hear her short gasps of breath, feel the warmth of it, of her mouth on me.

"Look at me."

I feel her shake her head.

"Look at me."

"I can't."

"You will."

I take a handful of hair, forcing her head backward because I want to see her. I want to hear her breath catch. I want to hold her against the cold, dirty wall and watch her take it, take my cock inside her as I own her.

She makes another sound, a small whimper. Her mouth opens and she's clinging to me and I fuck her virgin pussy, and she feels so good. So fucking good.

Her breathing changes and she's watching me now and the sounds she makes, small and desperate, they make me want to get closer. Deeper.

And when she gasps deeply and her pussy throbs around my cock, I thrust one last time, burying myself inside her, my cock throbbing, emptying, filling her up as she whimpers at my neck, her body going limp against mine, her full weight in my arms.

I hold her like this for a long time. I feel her holding me, and when I set her down, her knees buckle and I catch her, look down at her, feel the come and the blood on my dick.

She stares up at me, breath shallow, arms useless at her sides.

I pull up my jeans, see the smear of blood on my dick, see it on her wet thighs. I meet her eyes.

"You came, Amelia" I say.

No words.

"Know that I know what you want. I know who you are."

I can't read her eyes. It's too dark in here. But I know if I pull away, she'll fall. I think she's only standing because of the wall at her back and me at her front.

So when I do draw back, I scoop her up and she doesn't fight me and when we get upstairs, I sit her on the edge of the tub and fill it with warm water before setting her inside it.

She closes her eyes, hangs her head, then pulls her knees up and makes fists of her hands and presses the heels against her eyes.

I watch her for a long minute before stripping off my jeans and climbing into the large tub, facing her. I pull her hands from her eyes because I want to watch her cry.

And when she looks up at me, accusations make her eyes burn.

"You don't know me, Gregory Scafoni. You don't know anything about me. You have no idea who I am."

10

AMELIA

The sun is just beginning to rise and I'm still awake. I don't sleep at all that night, apart from those hours in the living room. Maybe it's jet lag. I'm not used to the time difference yet. Maybe it's that I don't want to have that dream again.

But if I'm honest with myself, I know those aren't the reasons.

My body aches. I feel raw inside and out. My back is scratched up from the wall. My insides, from him.

I should have made him stop.

Could I have?

I should have fought.

Told him to go to hell, but instead, I clung to him. I pulled him closer.

What he said, at least part of it, it's true. I wanted him last night.

I want this.

But he's wrong if he thinks he knows me, and I have found his weakness. He gave it away last night.

Helena.

She's his weakness.

And I hate him a little for that.

Maybe I hate her a little too and this, this knowledge shames me.

Whatever happened on that island, it broke him.

He thinks this is his revenge, but I don't think it's revenge he wants. It's more than that.

Her?

No. I can't think about that.

He's holding me. His arm is heavy around my waist and my back is to his front and he's breathing evenly. I think he's asleep.

The deep orange light of the sunrise streams through the split in the curtains and I look down at his hand on my belly. At the glove on it.

He never took it off, not even when we were in the bath. I touch it lightly, so lightly I don't think he'll feel it.

It's made of the softest, finest leather. I wonder if he's so used to it, he doesn't even notice it anymore. I want to know what's underneath. What is so horrible that he won't let anyone see it.

I don't know why I asked him if he was in love with Helena. Hearing the words out loud, it was jarring. Knowing they came from me, strange. How they made me feel, wrong.

What do I want? What have I wanted all along? This?

Have I truly wanted this all along?

Did I really want a Scafoni bastard to come and take me, to make me a Willow Girl?

I don't want to think about this. Not now. But when I try to scoot out from under his arm, he pulls me closer.

Was I wrong? Has he been awake all this time?

"We're not finished yet." His deep voice rumbles against my neck, making every hair stand on end. He rubs his chin against me, the scruff on his jaw rough.

I feel him behind me. Feel him hardening.

With a small sound of protest, I try to break free because I should break free.

But he holds tight, rolling me onto my stomach, laying his full weight on me, spreading my legs with his, dragging my arms over my head and gripping my wrists in his hands.

"Tell me who you are, Amelia Willow," he says at my ear. "I am so damn curious."

I tense up when he begins to slide into me. I'm still sore from last night and fighting my own want.

He moans, licks the curve of my shoulder, closes his mouth over it and bites.

I gasp at the sensation of his teeth on me, sinking

into me. I wonder if he'll draw blood but he's careful not to break skin.

He moves inside me, and I'm stretching for him, my body accommodating him. Wanting him.

"Tell me again how you don't want me."

He shifts my hands into one of his and slides the other to my hip and it's suddenly cold when he lifts his weight off my back.

Moving the hand that was holding my wrists to the back of my head, he draws me up so I'm on my knees. When he grips my hips, I turn my cheek into the pillow and watch him behind me, between my legs, hands on my ass, spreading me open, looking at me there, looking at me take him.

When he meets my gaze, his eyes almost glow, black and shiny, and his mouth moves into a grin and he thrusts hard and it hurts but it feels good, so good.

"Tell me because all I see is a Willow Girl dying to be fucked."

It's his words that jar me, that feel like a fist to my belly.

"I hate you," I say, and when I try to pull away, he tightens his grip on me.

"No, you don't. You only wish you hated me."

He shifts his gaze back to my ass, and when I feel his finger at my asshole, I bolt upright. But I can't get away because his grip on my hips is too tight and he's still inside me.

He chuckles, and I'm leaning forward, hands flat against the headboard. The sensation of him inside me at this angle, it's different.

He shifts his grip, one hand spanning my belly, the other around my throat. He pulls me backward into him, my back to his front, and his thrusts are deliberate and deep.

I turn my face a little and he licks my cheek, kisses my ear.

"I'll fuck your tight little virgin ass too," he whispers.

"Fuck you."

"You'll come with my dick in your ass, Amelia. You'll beg for it."

I do hate him. I do.

But that hate, it's part of this wanting. It's what makes this burn so hot.

He slides the hand that's on my belly down to cup my pussy, to rub my clit and the scruff of his jaw scratches my neck and my breath hitches and as hard as I try not to, I'm going to come.

He tightens his hand around my throat.

I grip the headboard, my knuckles white, and let out a whimper. A moan.

"I like how you sound when you come," he whispers. "How you tense up and throb around my cock."

And it's like my body wants to do it, to give him what he wants, to be obedient, and I come and when I do, he pushes me forward on my hands and knees and his thrusts are hard and he thickens inside me and with one final thrust, he stills, coming, and when I turn my head to look at him, I see ecstasy on his face, I see perfect bliss.

Beautiful bliss.

And it's impossible to look away.

Moments later, when his eyes focus once again, he lies down on top of me, flattening me to the bed. He's still inside me and he kisses my cheek.

"Just a girl wanting to be fucked," he whispers, sliding out of me.

I pull my arms underneath myself and close my legs when I feel him spill out of me. I don't know what I expect, what I want but then he gets off the bed and he's gone, and the bathroom door closes, and the shower goes on and I just lie there in his bed and I feel so small. So very small.

His smell clings to me. It's all around me.

Our smell.

His stuff is inside me, sticky between my legs, and all I can do is stare at the light desperate to penetrate the heavy drapes.

But it can't and I'm trapped here in this half-light. We both are. Frozen in this winter-time.

What am I doing?

What do I want?

No, not what.

How?

How do I want this?

This.

Him.

How in hell do I want *him*?

Something swells inside me, something sad. A weight in my belly. A tangible, palpable thing. And all at once, my eyes fill up with tears and I just look at the windows as I let them fall. Feel them slide over the bridge of my nose and onto the pillow.

The shower switches off and a moment later, the bathroom door opens, and I don't want him to see me like this. But he walks around the bed, and he's wearing a towel low over his hips and those tattoos, they're a blur of dark ink on his chest, his arms, and we're still not finished.

He sits down on the edge of the bed.

I close my eyes.

He touches my cheek, tucks my hair behind my ear, and he's gentle. Opposite last night. Opposite this morning. It's easier when he's rough.

With the tip of his thumb, he smears a tear across my face.

"I think Willow Girls were made to cry," he says.

I don't look up at him.

More tears don't come.

And he gets up and walks away and a few minutes later, he's gone.

11

AMELIA

"I think Willow Girls were made to cry."

I let myself wallow for exactly five minutes after he leaves before I push the covers off and get up to shower. I can't just lie there feeling sorry for myself. Can't just let him beat me.

When I return to the bedroom, I find several bags of clothes and shoes waiting for me. Everything I could need for several weeks and all of it my size. I choose a pair of jeans and a warm wool sweater along with a pair of boots that reach up to my knees.

At the door, I hesitate, but steel my spine and open it to head downstairs.

I will not be some meek little doll. I won't break this easily.

Gregory is having coffee and reading the paper when I get to the dining room. He glances up when I enter, looks me over, nods once in approval then returns his attention to the paper.

I pour myself some coffee from the carafe and help myself to a croissant.

He thinks he knows me? Well, I know him too. I know his weakness.

I just have to find some to use it against him.

To make him feel the way he makes me feel.

He folds the paper and sets it aside.

"It's good manners to thank someone when you receive a gift."

"Excuse me?"

"The clothes."

"The clothes are not a gift. You kidnapped me, remember?" His face darkens, and I turn my attention to stirring cream into my coffee. "Besides, I didn't ask for a gift."

"Would you prefer to walk around naked? Because that can certainly be arranged."

I don't doubt it.

"Amelia?"

I turn to him. I glare. "Thank you."

"Don't mention it," he says, one side of his mouth curving upward into a smile.

Fuck. You.

"You should call your sister today."

I'm surprised by this. "Why?"

"She seems worried. She's been texting you."

He takes out my cell phone, which was in his

pocket, and slides it across the table to me.

"You read my messages?"

He shrugs a shoulder.

"When she finds out what you did, she'll come get me."

"Probably. But thing is, I don't think you're going to tell her. Because I don't think you want her to come get you."

I don't reply.

"Besides, I haven't collected all I paid for."

I shrink back, his words making me feel small.

"Would you have gone through with it? With a stranger?" he asks.

"Aren't you a stranger?" And doesn't that make me some sort of whore?

"We're different, you and me." Any mockery is gone replaced by something almost sad. "We were never strangers. History saw to that."

I watch him, and I think what beautiful poetry he makes. What terrible, beautiful poetry. And in that moment, I think I see him. I think I glimpse the man beneath the monster.

But it's gone as swiftly as it came.

And he's still every bit the monster.

He takes the phone back, scrolls through, pushes a button and puts it on the table between us.

When Helena answers on the second ring, he gives me a smirk.

"Amy? Where have you been? I've been trying to

call," she says over speaker.

"Oh." I'm unprepared.

"Are you okay? Is something wrong?"

I look at Gregory who's watching me so confidently. So much like he knows exactly what I'm going to say.

"Amy?"

"I'm fine, Helena. Sorry. I just..." I look down at the table.

"Where are you? Isn't it the middle of the night? Are you hurt? Did something happen?"

Shit. Time difference.

Gregory's grin bares every single one of his teeth.

I move to swipe the phone off the table and take it off speaker, but he catches my wrist, shakes his head.

"Amy? What's going on?"

"I'm fine. Everything's fine," I say. "I got this last-minute job...um...in France. Another girl got sick, so my agent sent me in her place."

"France? Where in France?"

"Oh. Uh. Paris."

"You're in Paris and didn't tell me?"

"It was all very last minute, and I've been so busy, and I..." I think. "I needed to buy a new charger for my phone since mine is the wrong kind..." I'm rambling and Gregory's enjoying every second of my discomfort. "The battery died."

"Well, how long are you there? It's only a short

flight. I'm sure the doctor—"

"No. You shouldn't come. I'm leaving again tomorrow. Flying back. I won't have time to see you."

"Well, can't you extend the trip and come to the island?"

I pause. She's so close, my sister. I can go to her right now. I can fly to Venice. I can take a train.

It's what I should do.

If I were sane, it's what I would do.

But I meet Gregory's eyes and I know I won't.

"No. I'm sorry. I have another job when I'm back."

"Wow," she pauses. "That's great, Amy. I'm glad it's working out for you."

Guilt twists my heart.

I'm a liar.

Strange that the only person I'm not lying to is my enemy.

"I have to go."

"You sure you're okay?" Helena asks. "You don't sound like yourself."

"Yeah. Just tired. I forgot to ask how you are."

"Fine. Tired too."

"I bet." I don't know what else to say.

"Amy..."

"I have to go. They're waiting for me. I'll call you again as soon as I can, okay?"

It's silent. I need to get off the phone. Helena knows me too well.

"Talk to you soon," I say.

"Bye."

I hang up, tuck the phone into the pocket of my sweater.

"What doctor?" Gregory asks.

I look at him and I wonder if he knows. If he knows that Helena is pregnant.

"I don't know," I lie.

He watches me, stands, walks behind my chair. He reaches into my pocket to take the phone.

"You're a good liar. Better than I expected you'd be."

I exhale.

He believed me that I didn't know about the doctor.

He turns the phone off, takes the battery out again then shoves it into his pocket.

Matteo walks in just then. He's wearing his coat and says something to Gregory in Italian.

Gregory replies, turns to me. "I'll be back later. If you need anything, Irina's here."

"Where are you going?" I ask.

"I have some things to take care of."

"Where?"

"Rome."

"Rome?"

He nods.

"Can I come?"

He stops, surprised, and I think he's going to

say no.

I stand, put my hands on my hips. "If you're going to keep fucking me, I probably should be sure my pills are up to date. Neither of us wants another Scafoni bastard underfoot, do we?"

I think I have him.

I give him a smirk, give myself a mental pat on the back.

His posture relaxes, he cocks his head to the side. "You get the birth control shot. You just had it three weeks ago."

My smile vanishes.

His grows.

"I'm not stupid, Amelia. I wouldn't come inside you if there was any chance of making a Willow whore."

I think I physically flinch. How can this man's words do so much damage?

How can they so wound me?

"At least we agree on that then," I say, having to force myself to hold his gaze even though my voice sounds weak.

We stand there for a long awkward minute before he finally speaks. "Finish your breakfast."

Is that a yes?

I stick the last of my croissant—okay, the remaining half—into my mouth.

"Done," I say quickly, not wanting him to change his mind.

His eyebrows go up, but he doesn't say anything. Instead, he gestures for me to walk ahead of him and at the door, he picks up one of the coats hanging on the rack and holds it up for me. It's a long, gray wool coat with clasp buttons at the front. And it's a perfect fit just like the other things.

After he buttons it up, he puts on his own and we go outside where Matteo is waiting with the car.

It's good to go outside, although it's freezing. It's good to get out of that house.

The sun is bright, and snow is still blanketed under a layer of ice, everything frozen.

I watch as Matteo takes the steep curve down the hill, rocks crunching under the heavy tires of the SUV. We drive past a small village and eventually onto a highway that leads us to Rome.

The city is beautiful and bustling with tourists and locals. It's so much busier than I expect with traffic, car horns honking and people darting across streets I wouldn't dare to.

Matteo follows a few feet behind us, and Gregory has my arm which is a good thing because I'm sure I'd be run over by a car with all the gawking I'm doing at the ancient buildings and churches and squares that are just the norm here.

"I've never seen anything like this," I say.

Gregory stops and looks at me and looks around me like he's seeing it differently for the first time.

He has no idea how lucky he is to have grown up

surrounded by all of this history. It must have been so exciting, thrilling.

"Just take care not to get hit by a car."

"Would you be sad?"

He grins. "Matteo will take you to get what you need."

I glance at Matteo and I don't know why it matters, why I should care if it's Gregory or Matteo. Both are my jailors, aren't they?

What was it he'd said that night at the bar? Devil you know?

"Where are you going?" I ask.

He puts his finger on the tip of my nose like I'm a child. "Curious little Willow Girl."

"Stop calling me that. I'm not the Willow Girl."

He grips my collar, pulls me to him, but it's not hard, just abrupt. "Be good. Do as Matteo says, or I'll punish you, do you understand?"

The excitement I felt at being here dissipates and I nod my head.

"Matteo," he says, not taking his eyes off me, releasing me, adjusting my coat. "Take her where she needs to go."

He nods, and Gregory is about to walk away, and I hate this but I clear my throat. He checks his watch, raises his eyebrows.

"I don't have any money."

"Matteo will take care of it."

I raise my chin up, my lips tightening. I hate this.

He steps toward me. "What do you say, Amelia?" he taunts.

I grit my teeth. "Thank you, Gregory."

He smiles then walks off, disappearing into the crowd.

I look up at Matteo who doesn't seem at all uncomfortable or put out at having to babysit me.

"Is there a pharmacy?" I ask.

He nods, and we walk a few blocks to a pharmacy where I spend about forty-five minutes looking at things I don't need because pharmacies here are very different than what I expect. I buy some essentials and decide on some non-essentials too, lip gloss, mascara, eye liner. A little cover up because I'm starting to look like a racoon from the lack of sleep.

When we're done, I see the hairdresser around the corner, and I have an idea.

Instantly, a very loud warning voice inside my head screams no. Screams it would be stupid to taunt him. That I'd be asking for his wrath.

But my legs carry me in, and Matteo follows me to the door where I stop him.

"I need to fix this," I say, pointing to my hair. "It'll probably take a little time. Like an hour or maybe more. So why don't you go get some coffee or something. There." I point to a café across the street.

He gives me a smirk much like Gregory's. "Nice try."

I suck in a frustrated breath. "Just wait outside then. I'm not going to run away. I have nowhere to go and no money, remember? And I don't need a babysitter."

"I need a smoke anyway," he says.

That works just fine.

I walk inside and it's a small place with one older woman in a chair having her hair rolled into curlers and a hairdresser reading a magazine behind the counter.

She looks up when I enter, and I go to her.

"Can you fix this?" I ask gesturing to the back of my hair, which is crooked. I literally had gripped a handful of it and cut it straight across the night I'd colored my hair.

She looks at it, says something in Italian and gestures for me to take a seat.

"Also, I'd like a little color."

I pick up a hair color magazine and point to what I want, where I want it on my head. She clearly thinks it's a bad idea but shrugs a shoulder and we begin.

I can see Matteo in the reflection of the mirror. He's busy on his phone and smokes two cigarettes in a row, looking back to check that I'm still there every few minutes. I give him a grin and a wave. After he's finished with his cigarettes, he comes into the salon and takes a seat, still busy on his phone.

But it doesn't matter if he's here. He has no idea

what I'm doing. I wonder if he was even on the island. If he knew Helena or even saw her.

About an hour and a half later, the girl tugs my smock off with a flair. "Voila," she says, and I get a look at it. Turn my head a little to check the color.

It's perfect.

At a quick glance, I could be her.

I ignore the sinking feeling in my belly and get to my feet. "I love it," I tell her.

Matteo stands too, is clearly confused with my choice in color, but pays the girl and we leave.

He checks his watch.

I'm biting my lip, wondering if I should buy a hat. Second guessing myself.

"Mr. Scafoni will be finished in a few minutes."

I turn to Matteo. "*Mr. Scafoni* can wait a little longer. I need a few more things."

I walk ahead of him into the art supply store I spy a few shops away. Inside, I pick up two new sketchbooks—mine are full—and some pencils.

At the cash register, they have a rack of berets. They're felt, not real hats, or not meant to be worn as such. There's a fat, mustached cartoon character painting a scene wearing one of the berets, but I don't understand the text. Still, I pick one up, cut off the tag and set it on the counter and tuck my hair into the hat, ignoring that same voice inside my head now calling me chicken.

"Now I'm finished," I say after Matteo pays.

"Although I am hungry."

He rolls his eyes. "Let's go." He takes my arm and I follow, carrying my two bags. A light snow has begun to fall again, just some flurries, but it feels even colder than before.

It takes us fifteen minutes to get to a tiny street, almost an alley, that is utterly quiet compared to the rest of the city. There, in the far corner is a small tattoo parlor.

Matteo opens the door and I walk in and it's deeper than it looks, and quite dark. Music screams from the loudspeaker and I realize what his appointment is. What he's been doing.

My face grows serious when I see him at the back. He must have seen me when I walked in because his dark gaze is intent on me.

If it hurts, he doesn't show it. I've never had a tattoo, so I don't know.

I take a step toward the back. I want to see. But Matteo catches my arm.

"He's almost finished. Sit down."

I tug my arm free and don't sit.

We just keep watching each other, Gregory and I, my skin prickling under his intense gaze.

The girl who's working on him says something, glances up at me. I instantly don't like her. She's beautiful, with long black hair and full sleeve tattoos on both arms and even little colorful stars at one temple.

He replies to her and then, a few minutes later, he's finished.

He stands, looks back at his shoulder in the mirror, still too far for me to see.

She points something out and they have a quick conversation as she places something over the tattoo to protect it.

I want to see. I'm desperate to.

I wonder what I can exchange for him to let me see.

But then I remember what I did, what's under the felt beret. I touch the thick, blow-dried strands and watch him hand the girl a stack of bills before returning his gaze to me as he pulls on his shirt.

The girl tucks the money into her back pocket, and I feel a pang of jealousy because she knows this other part of him, this intimate and very personal part.

He walks toward me, and I can't help my gaze from dropping to the lines of muscle on his hard belly, his sculpted chest and I feel my face heat up as I remember how we were this morning.

Him behind me.

Holding me.

Inside me.

When I meet his eyes, he narrows his and I know he knows what I'm thinking.

He doesn't say anything apart from complimenting my hat, though.

I touch it, adjust it, trying to hide the silver strands beneath it.

"Thank you."

He puts his coat on, the silence between us heavy.

"You have everything you need?" he asks.

I nod, not quite looking at him.

"You got a tattoo." I wonder if he'll be covered head to toe in ink when he's finished.

He puts his coat on, walks to me as he buttons it.

"You fixed your hair," he says, and I have no choice but to face him.

I see the change in his eyes instantly.

His big hand cups a handful of hair, dark and light all in the same grip. I stare up at him, but his eyes are on that silver streak, and then he's dragging the beret off my head and more hair is falling into his hand and I think this was a really bad idea. The very worst idea.

He meets my eyes and my belly feels strange, like a brick has just dropped inside it.

He fists the beret in his hand and wraps his gloved one around the back of my neck, turning me roughly toward the door and I can feel his anger growing and all I can do is hug my bags to myself and stumble along with him as his grip tightens.

I open my mouth to say something once we're outside, the flurries having turned to a proper, heavy snow, but my throat is dry, and I can't speak.

He doesn't speak either. He just walks me swiftly to the car, and once we're there, sets me in the backseat and fastens my seatbelt but he doesn't sit next to me. Instead, he rides in the front with Matteo, arguing with him in Italian and I think I probably got Matteo into trouble too.

The car ride is the longest and my stomach is churning as we near the house. I'm hoping he's slightly calmer by the time we get there, but the instant Matteo parks the SUV, Gregory is out pulling my door open.

He gestures for me to step out and I can feel the rage rolling off him. His silence is a too-thin mask for what's beneath.

It takes me a few tries to undo my seatbelt and he takes my arm before my feet even touch ground as I slide out of the SUV and we rush inside where I barely acknowledge the warmth of the fire as we enter. He walks me briskly up the stairs, still not saying a word, not looking at me.

Only when we get to his room does he release me.

I stumble away when he does, rubbing my arm.

He gives me one hard look before going into the bathroom, and I'm confused but then he's back a moment later and he's holding a pair of scissors.

"What are you doing?" I back away from him as he approaches slowly, almost calmly. But he's not calm. Not even a little bit.

The scissors glint, sharp in his hand.

"I don't know who you are?" he asks.

My back hits the wall. "What are you doing with those?"

"I know exactly who you are." He reaches out, takes hold of a handful of my hair, the newly colored locks.

I grip his wrist. "Don't!"

He tugs the hair. "What were you thinking to do this? That you'd fuck with me somehow?"

"Why does it fuck with you? I mean, if you're not in love with her, why does it fuck with you?"

He pulls me to him by that lock of hair so my head is bowed at a strange, almost subservient and painful angle.

"Do you want to be her?" he asks, and he doesn't wait for me to answer.

I let out a scream when I hear the sound of those sharp blades closing, watch the strands of silver and black hair slipping from his fingers.

"Stop!" I try to drag him off, to stop him. I think he's going to butcher it, cut off all my hair and I'm just vain enough to be scared. To be fucking terrified.

But he steps away, releasing me, and we're both looking at that handful of hair, at that silver and black, and he releases it and it floats to the floor and we watch it fall to our feet and I'm touching my head, the short stubble of hair on the one side.

He looks up at me and I know he's not finished.

I back away.

He drops the scissors to the floor, and I realize I'm crying, and I think he's right. I am weak.

Without a word, he comes to me and his eyes are fierce, almost completely black.

Just like the night before, he grips my face, squeezes my cheeks and it hurts and I wonder if I'll have bruises tomorrow.

His other fist slams into the wall beside my head and I'd scream but I can't open my mouth and I'm sobbing now and shaking and fucking terrified.

"Don't think you can fuck with me," he spits. "Don't ever think you can fuck with me."

He squeezes my face hard once more before releasing me, stepping backward, eyes still on me and I think it takes all he has to do that, to walk away.

To not hurt me.

And as I sink to the floor, he just watches me and he's stepping on that pile of silver hair, my hair.

Hers.

Like hers.

And he looks down just for a second, just a split second and then he's gone, and the door slams shut, and I hear the lock turn and I just stay there, on my knees, hugging my arms to myself, trying to stop the shaking.

Trying to breathe.

12

GREGORY

I lied.

She can fuck with me.

She did fuck with me.

She knew exactly what button to push.

It took all I had to walk out of that room. And locking her in, it was as much to keep her safe as to punish her. Maybe more. The rage I felt at seeing what she'd done, I'm not sure I could have controlled it. Controlled myself.

This taunt, this knowing, calculated taunt, what the fuck was she thinking?

And why the fuck am I so affected? That's the important question here.

But fuck, the timing. The girl at the tattoo parlor mentioned who was in town. Mentioned he'd been looking for me. I don't know what business he has with me, but he's gone to some trouble to make sure I know he's here.

I shake my head, look around the empty room.

At least she's upstairs.

At least the house isn't empty.

It's late afternoon and a heavy snow is falling outside. Inside it's warm, though, and I'm sitting in the living room in front of the fire, watching it. The curtains are drawn to match my mood.

Matteo didn't know, I get that, but fuck.

I take a swig of whiskey straight from the bottle. I gave up on the glass about an hour ago. My back, behind my shoulder, throbs. The tattooed skin is tender. I should take care with it, but I press it into the back of the chair.

Pain.

More pain.

More to come. My back is unfinished.

I look at my gloved hand. Curl it into a fist. Uncurl it.

"Were you in love with her?"

Did she ask the question innocently? I think she did. I don't think Helena told her anything. If she had, Amelia would have more ammunition.

But as innocent as her question was, my response was telling.

I force myself to think about her.

Helena.

Sebastian sharing her with me. Never giving her wholly. Controlling every touch. Every breath.

And me going along with it.

Why the fuck did I go along with it?

I think about her that night in the kitchen at Lucinda's house. I think that's the night that wounded me most. That was the night of true betrayal. The branding, that was just me not having sense enough to see what was so painfully clear all along.

But am I or was I in love with her?

I think about this. I force myself to.

Growing up, Sebastian thought he had it hardest. But I don't know if he realized how fucked up it is when it's your own mother who casts you aside.

He wasn't Lucinda's biological child, and, in a way, I can see her hatred of him. He blocked the path to what she wanted. He stood as a symbol of how she was never first, not for our father, not when it came to her sister, not when it came to the Willow Girl, not when it came to her step-son.

I'm trying to remember if she loved Ethan more after the accident.

Accident.

I snort.

What a joke. I knew what Sebastian had done all along.

I saw his guilt on his face.

With Ethan, she had her first-born son. Something of tremendous value to the Scafoni family. I guess I was a sort of back-up plan. The spare.

A log rolls out of the fire and onto the hearth.

I stand up, go to it. Push it back in with the toe of my shoe. I lean against the mantle and look at the burning flames.

Why the fuck am I sitting here feeling sorry for myself? Because who gives a fuck that my mother didn't love me. Fuck that. I don't care. I never have.

And I think Helena's rejection of me, her choosing Sebastian, maybe it was just an extension of what I've known all along.

Never the one anyone wanted.

Never the one anyone chose or loved.

"Jesus Christ."

I'm fucking pathetic.

I drink, swallowing the last gulps of whiskey. I set the bottle on the mantle and go to the stairs, pausing there. Looking up.

Everything is different with her and I don't know why that is and I didn't think it would be this way. It's like having her here now, it makes things different. Not so pointless or empty.

I take a step, stumble, stop. I should leave her be. For tonight, I should leave her be.

But I can't.

I climb the stairs, walking where the banister should be, looking down at the stone floor.

One slip, one step missed, and I'd go down.

I exhale, tucking my hand into my pocket for the key, not moving away from the edge even when I stumble on the last step.

Remarkably, I'm silent when I walk down the hall toward my room. Like one of the ghosts who haunts this house.

I pause at the door. Listen. There's no sound from inside. I unlock it, push the door open.

She's sitting on the floor, her back against the foot of the bed, a sketch book open on her knees, pencil in hand.

She looks over at me, and she looks like she's been crying for days.

Short silver stubs of hair are sticking out from where I cut the strands, but she's picked up the hair off the floor and the scissors are gone.

I go to her, see how her grip tightens on the pencil she's holding.

I sit on the edge of the bed. Look down at what she's sketched. Not that I need to. I know what it is.

She looks down at it too.

A tear drops from her cheek to the sketchbook, the blob smearing the lead.

She wipes it away with the tip of her finger and watches the stain spread to the end of the page.

She can't seem to stop drawing that night any more than I can stop tattooing it on my skin.

The night of the reaping fucked with all of us.

I don't think any of us realized it then.

The night their parents made them wear those rotting sheaths we demanded of them, the night they put their daughters on those blocks for the first-born Scafoni son to take his pick... No one knew that it would break us. Tear us all apart.

I look down at the book.

This particular sketch, it's different than the others.

She lays her hand flat over the part I'm most interested in, hiding it from me.

I reach down, close mine over hers, look at the difference in our hands. Mine huge. Gloved. Hers small. Pale.

If only she knew the ugliness beneath that leather.

I move her hand away.

She usually draws Sebastian. Sebastian and Helena.

But this one, it's me. It's me standing where Sebastian stood looking at the girl on the block. But she's drawn horns coming out of my head. A goat's horns.

Or Satan's.

I laugh—it's a strange sort of chuckle and maybe it's the alcohol because it's not funny, not when you look at the eyes. Eyes so full of emotion it's like I can feel what she's feeling, what she felt when she drew it.

It's the thing that throbs all around her like a

living, breathing entity. Like it's sucking air out of the room. Like it's syphoning the life out of her.

Longing.

That's what it is.

She longs.

We both do.

And this hunger, it will devour us both.

The girl on the block, I can't tell who it is. I don't know if it's Helena or Amelia in front of me. Because now, with her dark hair, they look so similar and either she drew it so they're indistinguishable or I'm fucking drunk and everything is fuzzy.

I let go of her wrist, peer down, wanting to see. Wanting to know.

Another fat tear drops heavy onto the page and this time when she lays the flat of her hand on it, it's to swirl the wet across it like maybe she can wipe away that night. Smear it off the page. Smudge it out of the past.

"Don't," I say.

She doesn't listen though. She rubs more tears from her eyes and smears them around the page, destroying it.

"Why do you keep drawing it?"

"I don't know."

She stops.

I wait.

"So I can erase it," she says, her voice quieter. "Stop it from ever happening."

"Why did you do that? Color your hair like hers?"

She turns her head, looks up at me. Her eyes are puffy, red from crying. "Maybe the same reason you get the tattoos." She wipes her face, leaving a smear of pencil on her cheek, and goes quiet again.

"I don't love her." It's the first time I've said those words out loud and it's a relief because I think they're true. Even drunk as I am, I think they're true.

She shifts her gaze back to mine again.

"Let me see," she says.

"What?"

"Take off your shirt. Let me see them."

I shake my head.

One corner of her mouth curves upward but it's more sad than anything else.

"You're obsessed with her and you don't even know it."

"You're wrong."

"Prove it." She puts the notebook down, turns so she's kneeling between my knees facing me, her hands on my thighs. "Show me. Show me what they did to you."

Her words strike me. Make me stop.

"Show me what they did to you."

I keep looking at that sheet of paper. At the mess of black and white and gray like the destruction a hurricane would leave behind, and I feel this thing inside me, and I want it gone. I just want it gone.

"They made a monster out of me." I almost don't recognize the strange, broken voice.

She studies me and if she sees my back, she'll know what happened on that island. She'll know everything. Or most everything. The tattoos aren't finished yet.

"Show me. Please."

Maybe it will make it easier if I do.

Maybe I can deal with it then. Show her. Let her see. Own it instead of letting it own me.

"What will you give me in exchange?" I ask.

She considers this, averting her gaze, biting her lip. I watch her.

When she looks back at me, I think how much I like her eyes.

How different she is to what I first thought.

How she's so much more.

Maybe it's our shared longing that makes her so. That makes me see her so.

She inches closer, and her hands feel warm on my legs and I just sit there because she's never touched me before. Not willingly. Not really.

I look down at them, at her small hands, fragile wrists. Look back at her face. Even puffy from crying and smeared with pencil, she's beautiful, but so much more. So much more than some genetic lottery.

"What will you give me in exchange?" I ask

again, and I think something's changed between us. Just now, something is different.

She swallows. The room is so quiet, I hear it.

She leans forward, and I stay still, and she touches her lips to mine. Just touches them, almost a tickle, it's so light.

I remain as I am, and I let her.

I don't touch her.

I don't make her.

Don't force her.

And she kisses me.

When she pulls back, her cheeks are flushed. I reach out, put my hand flat over her heart. Feel the drumming of it, the rapid staccato of beat after beat.

She does the same, lays her hand over my heart, and her touch, it's electric. It's going to burn me up. Make ash out of me.

"I'll give you anything you ask for," she says.

"I can take anything I want."

"But what you want most is for me to give it to you."

Fuck.

This girl.

Fuck.

"On my terms," I say. I need to keep control of this. Of her.

After a moment, she nods.

I cup the back of her head, pull her to me. I kiss her, kiss her my way, and she opens for me. *For me.*

And I taste her, touch my tongue to hers and I want to devour her. I will. I pull her closer, but it won't ever be close enough because this kiss, this one, it's everything. Every single thing.

When I break the kiss, she's breathless.

So am I.

Releasing her, I unbutton my shirt down to my navel, open it.

Amelia's eyes are on my chest, and I can't read her expression. She's taking care with it.

She reaches out, touches me, and her fingers, they burn my skin where she traces the first and biggest tattoo. This one, it's familiar to her. It's her sketch. Four blocks. Four Willow Girls. Two blurred. Two clear. One bound.

And candles.

A thousand candles.

Ghosts hanging in the corners, smudges of dirty white, of shade so scant, they're almost nonexistent.

I remember the tattoo artist's face when she first saw the sketch. When I told her what I wanted.

Amelia follows the ink across the expanse of my chest, my shoulders, my arms, a skull, the mausoleum, the wings of a half-broken angel, a watcher, the whipping post.

Empty.

For now.

It's different on my back.

She spends the next fifteen minutes studying

every inch of my chest and arms with her eyes, her fingers and I feel every moment of it, every touch, every light tickle of her fingertips.

Why am I giving her this?

She takes hold of my shirt, pushes it off my shoulders, working slowly, letting me feel her hands on me. She's tender, cautious, different than how I touch her.

She rises to her feet to move behind me, but I'm not ready to give her that yet. I capture her wrists. Stop her.

"I want—"

I shake my head. "It's enough."

"We agreed."

"My terms."

"But—"

"You can't unsee things, Amelia."

She looks at me, her expression confused.

I release her, get up, pull my shirt back over my shoulders and walk to the door. I'm tired.

"What do you want?" she calls out from behind me.

I look at her, walk back to her, squint to see the faint bruises forming on her jaw. My fingerprints.

Only mine.

Because she's mine.

All mine.

My own Willow Girl.

No.

No, not that.

More than that.

She remains kneeling up, looking at me and I see us like this, me looming over her, her on her knees before me and all I can think is she's doomed because I'm never going to let her go.

Never.

"What do you want?" she asks again, confused. Maybe a little disappointed. "Our exchange."

Everything. Doesn't she know that yet?

I turn to walk to the door.

"Gregory?"

I stop. I don't look back.

"I'll collect later."

13

AMELIA

I'm still trying to make sense of what I did when I wake up the following morning. It's almost like I've been thinking about it all night. Like the thought is just continuing. When I kissed him like that, he seemed almost shocked by it. I know I was.

And then, what he did. Putting his hand over my heart.

And what I did. Putting mine over his.

I shake my head, flutter my eyelids open and I realize I'm not alone.

I don't know when he came into the bed but he's beside me now and I'm tucked into his chest. He's holding me and he's warm and I can't even remember if I dreamt.

But when I realize what I'm doing, how I'm

curled into him, I try to pull away, but his arm tightens around me.

"You talk in your sleep," he says, and he sounds like he did before last night. Like the door that was, for the briefest moment, open, is, once again, locked and barred.

"I don't."

I push against him, and he lets me roll onto my back. I turn to him, find him watching me, see the book in the hand that wasn't holding me.

"How long have you been awake?" I ask.

"A little while." He puts the book aside and his gaze travels to my chest and I look down. I'm wearing a tank top and pajama shorts, but I still pull the blanket higher. "I didn't want to wake you. You didn't settle down until the sun came up."

"I'm just not used to it here yet. What time is it?"

"Eleven."

I sit up, rub my eyes. It must be the time difference.

He watches me and I look at him, at his wide shoulders, the tattoos there, my gaze falling on the broken wings of the angel whose face is hidden behind more ink and it's strange to see that. Familiar, almost. He moves to sit up and my gaze shifts to the hard ripple of muscles on his belly. Seeing him like this, it makes my mouth water. It makes me want.

I swallow, clear my throat because when I look at

his eyes, I know he knows what I'm thinking. I know he knows his effect on me.

"I want something," I say, pushing that thought aside, because I have an idea.

"Do you?" He grins.

"It's not what you think." I roll my eyes, try to make light of it. I start to sit up.

"That's too bad," he says, climbing on top of me. "Lie down."

"This isn't..." I push against him, but I can't get out from beneath his weight.

"You should sleep naked from now on," he says, stripping me.

"Stop."

"Spread your legs," he says, looking at me.

"Gregory—"

"You want it. You know you do so spread your legs."

I look back at him and when I hesitate, he takes hold of my thighs, pushes them wide, pinning them to the bed, and looks down at me. At my sex. He dips his head low and licks the length of me and I gasp.

"You taste good," he says, meeting my eyes.

"I..." But he's licking me again, and I don't know why I go to pull him off me. It's the last thing I want, but he stops me anyway. He grabs my wrists holds them apart and circles my clit with his tongue before taking it between his lips and sucking.

I can't speak. I can hardly breathe. All I can do is

make this strange sound, like it's coming from deep inside my chest, and I find myself arching my back, pushing myself into him.

But, abruptly, just when I'm moments from coming, he stops, gives me a wide grin and kneels up between my legs. He bends my knees and pushes them way up so I'm spread wide.

I try to pull away, try to pull free of him.

"Look at me," he says.

I can't, though. Not when he's holding me like that, spread and open to him. Everything exposed to him.

"I said look at me," he repeats, this time, slapping my hip, making me gasp.

I turn my head.

"This is me collecting from last night," he says, and purposefully, he looks down at me, down at my sex, at everything. "I told you once that I want all of it, everything," he says, dipping his head again. "Your pussy." He licks me there, raising his head again. "Your ass." He slides his tongue from my pussy to my asshole, circling it, licking me there, too.

I'm mortified, and I turn my face away, but it feels good too, him licking me, all of me. I'm humiliated and I'm going to come all at once and he knows it. He knows it.

"Please."

He rises up, takes my arms and spreads them wide and pushes into me.

"Give it to me, Amelia. You promised me anything I want, and what I want is everything. Give it to me."

He twines his fingers with mine and lays his weight on me and kisses me and I taste myself on his lips, his tongue and our fucking is loud, the sounds of us together, our breathing, our sex, wet and hard and deep.

"Give it to me."

"I don't know how," I say finally, and he looks down at me and watches me like the last thing he expected was for me to say this.

"Then I'll take it until you figure it out." He's suddenly angry and the fucking is punishing and his cock grows bigger and it hurts and it feels so good and I want to give it to him. I want to.

But some part of me, it resists him, wants to fight him and he feels that too and he's holding me down and fucking me and I'm coming. I'm coming so hard I can't breathe and all I see of him is a blur and maybe this is it. Maybe this is me giving it to him. Maybe this is the way it has to be with us.

When my orgasm finally subsides and I can see clearly again, he's watching me, his eyes dark and intense on mine and he gives me a smirk, raises himself up and sweat falls from his forehead onto my face as he fucks me harder yet, fucks me to hurt me and all I can do is watch him and he's so incredibly beautiful.

So fucking beautiful.

And when he comes, his eyes, they're hard and soft at once, glowing almost, and his face…I can look at him like this forever and never get enough.

Never enough.

When he finally collapses on top of me, we're covered in sweat and panting for breath.

"Is this how it always is?" I ask and as soon as the words are out, they sound stupid and I wish I could take them back

But then he answers and maybe it's not stupid at all. "No." He studies me and sometimes it's like he sees right inside me. "Never before."

I blink, look away. I can't hold his gaze. It's too much.

"Tell me what you want," he says finally.

"What?"

He pushes sweat soaked hair off my face. "What do you want?"

It's almost tender how he touches me. Like he's being careful. Opposite how he is when he fucks me.

"Why do you do that?" I ask.

"Do what?" he asks.

I think. "Sometimes it's like I see you beneath your anger. But then, it's there again and you're this other person and I don't know what I'm supposed to do."

He doesn't quite meet my eyes, but traces fingertips over my face, my chin, neck, down to my breast.

I'm ready for him to hurt me, but he just caresses me and watches me.

"Tell me what you want," he says again.

I watch him too and I wonder if he, too, doesn't know how to be.

"A tattoo," I say.

"A tattoo?" He looks genuinely confused. Maybe disappointed. "Why?"

"I've always wanted one but wasn't allowed. The woman who does yours does good work."

"She does."

"Can you take me there?"

He gets out of the bed. "Why don't you think about it for more than twelve hours and I'll see." He disappears into the bathroom.

I push the covers back, follow him. I almost open the door but catch myself.

"It's not something I've only thought about for twelve hours. And I'm not asking your permission. I'm asking for a ride. Or, or...bus fare."

I hear his chuckle before the shower goes on.

"Jackass," I mutter, going back to the bed, pulling on my panties and tank top before sitting down.

He's done a few minutes later and returns to the bedroom. He gets dressed before coming back to the bed.

"What tattoo would you get? A heart? Some stars on your wrist? Isn't that some sort of trend?"

"You're such a jerk, you know that?"

He chuckles again. "I thought I was a jackass."

He heard that?

I get up, go through the stack of sketchbooks and find the one I want. It's an old one, one I brought from home. And every inch of every page is full.

Carrying it with me, I sit back down on the bed and open the book, turning through the pages until I get to it.

"Here," I say, pointing to the very corner of the sheet that's almost chaotic with all the drawings. "This one."

He comes over, peers down at it, then sits and takes the book out of my hands and I'm not sure he's as aware as I am of how close he is. How we're touching.

What that contact does to me.

"Where did you see this?" he asks after a few minutes.

"Nowhere. Just in my head."

He looks at me funny, like he doesn't quite believe me maybe.

"This bird, I see them everywhere. Even here in the library."

"In the library?"

I nod. I don't tell him that the same bird was in our library too. Not the same one, obviously, but the same type of bird. Watching us that night, the night of the reaping.

"She must have come in from a hole in the

window and couldn't get back out. I caught her, put her back outside."

"Did you?" he asks absently. His eyes are still intent on the picture.

"And this, it's an angel. See this, it's the shadow of her wing. It's almost like the wing of your angel."

His expression doesn't change, that crease between his eyebrows only deepens.

"Why is half her face a skull?"

"Because she's watching over the dead."

I hear myself say it, hear how matter-of-fact my voice sounds, how matter-of-fact my answer is, but how strange it is at the same time.

I take the book from his hands, close it.

"Never mind," I say, feeling suddenly very exposed, more exposed than I had been moments ago. Not liking the look on his face. "Forget it."

He stands, takes the book from me. "I'll take you tonight."

"Really?"

He nods, walks to the door. "Go get dressed. Have breakfast. I need to take care of some things today."

"Really? You'll take me?" I'm shocked.

"That's what I said."

"Will it hurt?" I ask when he reaches the door.

He turns, narrows his eyes. "You scared?" Jerk Gregory is back.

"No. I just want to know what to expect so I'm prepared."

"I think you'll appreciate the sensation."

※

WE DON'T HEAD INTO ROME UNTIL AFTER NINE THAT evening. The city is beautiful at night, although I'm too anxious about the tattoo to enjoy it. Gregory is sitting beside Matteo and they're speaking in Italian. I'm in the backseat clutching my sketchbook to myself and watching the scenery.

"You can change your mind," Gregory taunts once we park the SUV.

"I'm fine," I say, relaxing my hold on the book.

He'd also offered me some pills to numb any pain before we left the house, but I refused them. If I do this, I want to feel it. I want to feel every prick of the needle.

I button my coat as we get out of the car, Matteo lighting up a cigarette and following close behind as Gregory and I walk ahead.

"Why do you need a bodyguard?" I ask.

"A bodyguard?"

"Matteo."

"He's not a bodyguard."

"What is he then?"

Gregory shrugs a shoulder. "Anything I need him to be."

I recognize the alley-like street where the tattoo parlor is located. Apart from a few lights in the windows of the buildings and that of the parlor itself, it's pretty dark compared to the rest of the city.

"Are you sure she'll have time for me?" I ask.

He opens the parlor door and turns to me. "I booked her especially for you. But if you're rethinking it..." he trails off, taking hold of my collar, tugging me closer.

"I'm not chickening out."

"Good."

We walk inside and the place is empty but for the girl I recognize. She's leaning on the counter reading something on her phone and when she sees us, she smiles at Gregory then at me, takes the gum out of her mouth and throws it into a trashcan before sorting through the papers in front of her.

"Amelia, this is Laura, Laura, Amelia."

"Nice to meet you," I say.

She says the same and turns to Gregory, opening a folder beneath that stack of papers and laying out some sheets. They start speaking in Italian and I peer at the pages.

"How does she already have the drawing?" It's my drawing but she's sketched it bigger, placed it differently so it's longer with the bird tucked beneath the wing of the angel. Their wings are almost merged and the skull is less prominent, but there.

"I emailed it to her, told her what you were thinking." He stands aside, lays out the three different sketches, each just slightly different than the other.

"They're beautiful," I say, looking at each of them.

"You can change the color if you want," Gregory says.

The wings are darkest blue with hints of turquoise, that same turquoise that's in his eyes, and the bird's belly is red. And the angel herself, her face and arm, they look like they're made of stone. Of crumbling stone.

"It's perfect. Better than I imagined."

He nods.

"You did this?" I ask the girl.

She looks up at Gregory, starts to say something but Gregory cuts her off.

"Yeah. Laura's the best."

"Thank you," I tell her.

"Do you know where you want it?" he asks.

"Oh." I hadn't really thought about that. "Um..."

"Here?" he asks, turning me a little, touching the space along my upper back, my left shoulder blade, the curve of my arm. "What do you think?"

I look up at him and nod.

"It'll sort of trail off, like this," he shows me the edges of the drawing, like sand blowing away in a wind.

Like ash.

And it's so beautiful.

I'm overwhelmed and all I can seem to do is nod.

Laura straightens, takes the sketches. "Ready?" she asks.

Gregory is still watching me. He leans behind the counter to pick up a bottle of whiskey from a shelf underneath.

"Yes," I say, wanting some of that whiskey now. Thinking maybe I should have taken the pills he offered.

Gregory takes off his coat, hangs it up.

I follow Laura to the same seat where Gregory sat to have his done. I take off my coat and Laura tells me to straddle the chair so my back is to her. I do. It's comfortable and I can rest my head against the back of the seat. I unbutton my shirt, slide it off both arms.

"Bra too," she says.

I glance at Gregory who is watching from the other end of the parlor as I reach back to unhook my bra and take it off.

Laura positions me slightly differently. The leather feels cool against my bare breasts. She trains the light on the spot where the tattoo will go. The only sound is that of Gregory shoes as he walks toward us while she cleans the area, the antiseptic cold on my skin.

"It's okay," she says. She must see how nervous I am. "It will be so beautiful."

"Thanks."

Gregory comes closer, sets the bottle down, holds his glass out to me.

I look up at him, take it, drink a sip, hand it back.

He leans against the wall and Laura begins, the sound of the machine sounding much louder than it did the other day, sounding much scarier.

"Relax," Gregory says.

I take a deep breath in and uncurl my hands and close my eyes as she begins to work. And somehow, it's not unbearable, the sensation strangely satisfying. Almost.

The only sound is that of the needle buzzing for the next few hours until she's finally finished and she looks up at Gregory.

He peers closer and the intensity in his eyes as he watched for the entire three hours is only darker as he studies the tattoo, and, finally gives her a nod.

Laura takes a mirror and holds it out behind me, and I peer over my shoulder and my mouth falls open.

It's perfect.

It's beautiful.

No. More than that.

It's almost...alive.

And the blue of the angel's wings, it's the same blue as Gregory's broken angel.

"Do you like it?" she asks, her accent heavier. I think she must be exhausted.

"Yeah. It's..."

Laura smiles, nods at me like she gets it. I'm grateful because I can't seem to find words to describe what I see.

She stands, stretches, walks to another part of the shop.

I look up at Gregory and he shifts his gaze from the tattoo to me.

"Do you see ghosts, Amelia?"

The question is so abrupt and so out of place, that all I can do is stare stupidly up at him.

"That angel," he continues, "she stands watch over the Scafoni Mausoleum."

"What?"

"On the island."

"I don't understand."

"Neither do I," he says, the look in his eyes different. "How did you draw it?"

I just shake my head, trying to remember. It was just something I saw in my head.

"Did your sister tell you about it?"

"No. She doesn't talk about the island. Never has."

He shifts his gaze back to it.

"It's coincidence. Just an angel. That's all," I say.

But it's not. I know it. He knows it.

Like the ghosts of the dead Willow Girls hiding in the shadows of our library. Like the wraith-like smudges haunting the edges the tattoo on his chest.

"There's no such thing as coincidence, Amelia."

14

AMELIA

Gregory and Laura talk for a few minutes as I put my coat on. I can't understand what they're saying but I see how his face hardens. It's a brief conversation, though, and a few minutes later, we're walking out the door.

He makes two calls but both are in Italian so I can't follow. After that, he's discussing something with Matteo, and I don't think they're arguing but Gregory seems agitated. At one point, he even takes a cigarette from Matteo and cracks the window open to smoke it.

I'm tired so I lean my head back against the seat and look out the window. My shoulder feels tender and it's almost like the buzz of the needle is still vibrating through me.

By the time we get back to the house it's almost midnight and I've nodded off. I'm groggy for a moment when I wake and anxious to see the tattoo again, study it more closely. But I know something's wrong the moment we pull in through the gates.

"Fuck," Gregory mutters.

Someone's here. Three cars are parked along the circular drive around the broken-down fountain. They're black sedans, exact replicas of each other, with dark-tinted windows.

Tires crunch gravel as we slow and Gregory says something to Matteo, then turns to me.

"You'll go directly upstairs, understand?"

But I'm looking at the two men standing sentry on the steps leading up to the portico. Glancing at the light of a cigarette as another smokes along the kitchen entrance.

"What's happening?" I ask. "Who are they?"

He opens my door, takes my arm harder than he needs to and pulls me out. "It's too late to hide you. You'll go directly up to your room and you'll stay there until I come for you, am I clear?"

I look up at him and he doesn't look scared, just pissed off.

"I don't have a room," I stay stupidly.

"Christ."

Someone clears their throat and Gregory walks me toward the house. He eyes each of the two men standing on his front step, the third who opens his front door.

I look too, notice they're all dressed in dark suits. Notice that none meets our eyes.

"What's going on?" I whisper.

He squeezes my arm as we step inside, and Matteo is right behind us. Someone is talking, Irina's voice I recognize, the man's I do not. They're speaking in Italian and the man laughs heartily.

Gregory doesn't let me go, not for a second as he leads me into the house and toward the stairs, but they're visible to both the living and dining rooms so before he can rush me up, which I know is what he wants to do. The man who is talking to Irina stands from his crouched position at the fireplace, poker in hand, and turns to us.

He's tall, as tall as Gregory, and built roughly the same and he's wearing a dark suit too, but his is different than the others.

No, that's not it.

He just wears his differently.

His eyes scan me, taking me in from head to toe, pausing on the tightening grip Gregory has on my arm. He seems to takes a full minute before shifting his gaze to Gregory.

"Gregory," he says, smiling broadly, a smile that makes his face dimple on one side and that combined with his light hazel eyes, it makes him appear almost boyish and it's disarming because I know this man, he's no boy. I wonder if he ever was.

"Stefan," Gregory says, his voice calm and

controlled and I look up at him and think he, like this man, is dangerous, and for some reason, this knowledge, it makes me feel safer.

I look around, count the men I can see. Three. Three inside, three outside. And I can hear more upstairs.

"I heard you were back. Wanted to drop in and say hello."

"All the way from Palermo?"

The man, Stefan, gives him that smile again as he sets the poker down, brushes off his hands and shifts his gaze to me.

I notice Irina standing near the fireplace, her face paler than usual, eyes on Matteo.

Stefan walks toward us, openly lets his gaze slide over me.

I find myself drawing closer to Gregory as he shifts me slightly behind him.

"You have company," Stefan says.

"She was just going to bed," Gregory says.

I glance up at him and his eyes are hard, and I don't think he's blinked as he watches the other man's approach.

"That's too bad," Stefan says.

"Matteo," Gregory calls out.

Matteo is at his side in an instant and Gregory hands me over to him. "Take Amelia upstairs."

Stefan holds up his hand and a man steps forward to block our path.

"Amelia," he says like he's tasting my name and it makes the hair on the back of my neck stand on end.

He extends his hand, and when I don't move, he reaches to take one of mine and holds it in both of his and I look down and think how mine has all but disappeared, his are so big.

"Perhaps next time we'll have a few more minutes before your bedtime," Stefan says.

After what feels like forever, he releases me, and Matteo walks me hurriedly up the stairs. When I glance back, the two men are still standing there, Stefan watching me, Gregory watching him.

"Who are they?" I ask Matteo as he rushes me down the hall and into Gregory's room.

"Mafia," he says, opening the bedroom door, still not releasing me until he checks the room to make sure it's empty.

"Mafia?"

But by the time I ask it, he's out in the hallway, reaching around inside to take the key and when the door closes, I hear the lock turn and once again, I'm locked in.

15

GREGORY

After my first visit to the tattoo parlor, I knew it wouldn't be long before Stefan Sabbioni showed up at my door.

I study him.

He watches Amelia go, waits until she's out of sight to shift his gaze back to me.

"I like what you've done with the house," he says. He turns, walks into the living room, takes a seat like it's his house, not mine.

"I'm going to guess you already gave yourself a tour or I'd offer," I deadpan, taking the other seat.

"I hope you don't mind," he says. "I wasn't sure how long you'd be, and I was curious."

I just give him a half smile.

"It's a beautiful house. I'm glad Villa de Rossi has some new life in it." He doesn't give a shit about the house. "Amelia, was it?" he asks. "Pretty girl."

I don't answer. I don't like her name on his lips.

Irina, ever attentive, appears at my side with an empty glass. I notice how her hands tremble.

Stefan picks up the bottle of whiskey on the table between the two chairs. I guess he's helped himself to my whiskey too.

He pours me a glass. "I made myself at home."

"I see that."

He drinks his whiskey and I do the same, doing quick math, counting the half dozen men he's brought with him.

"Didn't realize you were able to leave Sicily these days," I comment.

He shrugs a shoulder. "My friends look the other way."

I've known Stefan Sabbioni ever since I can remember. He's a few years older than I am and our families have worked together in the past. He's one of four sons, of whom only he and his brother, Antonio, are still living as far as I'm aware. Several years ago, Antonio, the first-born and the one poised to take over the business, betrayed the family. He turned state's witness for the U.S.

Stefan's father was subsequently arrested and extradited. He never did make it to trial, though. He was murdered in prison.

Stefan took over the Sabbioni family after his father's arrest and extradition, but the family—and the American operation especially—had been severely weakened by his brother's betrayal.

For as long as I can remember, our families had had an understanding. Our business interests ran and still do run parallel in some cases, but they don't intersect. We're not the mafia.

I'm surprised to see Stefan here, outside of Sicily. It's worrying because it means he's regained some of their old power. Those friends who are looking the other way must be friends in high places because he's on a sort of house arrest. He's free to move about in Sicily. Free to operate there. But the rest of Italy is off limits.

Or so it was.

"What are you doing here, Stefan?"

He studies me. "Right to business with you."

"It's late."

"I imagine you want to get upstairs to your Amelia."

He winks like we're old friends. We're not.

I raise my eyebrows and wait.

He drinks a sip of his whiskey. "I like this brand," he says. "Used to be my brother's favorite too."

"Did it?" I could give a fuck.

"But who knows if he even drinks the stuff anymore."

"How can I help you, Stefan?"

He looks at me, the smile vanishing from his face, showing the hard man beneath.

"I have some business with Lucinda."

"Lucinda?" I ask, not having to feign ignorance because I haven't had contact with my mother in months. I know the deal Sebastian struck with her, but she and I, we aren't exactly close, never were, not even on the island. As far as I know or care, she's far, far away, and she can stay that way.

"She has something that belongs to me."

"And you either think she's here or that I know where she is which is why I assume you're here. Why you gave yourself a tour of my house."

"Well, that was secondary. I have always been curious about Villa de Rossi. Tell me, is it really haunted?"

"Only if you believe in ghosts."

He chuckles and we drink our whiskey, each of us watching the other. When he's emptied his glass, he sets it down and leans back in his chair.

"Lucinda, Lucinda," he chimes. "Any idea where I can find her?"

"My mother and I don't keep in touch. I don't even know which continent she's on."

"Really? Strange because I heard she's in town somewhere."

"Is she?"

"I assumed with you being back that she'd be here."

"You know what they say about making assumptions."

"Hmm," he pauses, nods his head like he gets my meaning. "She told me about Sebastian sending her away."

"She came to see you?" This surprises me. Please tell me Lucinda wasn't stupid enough to go to Stefan Sabbioni for help against Sebastian.

"Yes. She needed some help."

Fuck.

"Help with?" I ask, this time not ignorant of what she'd have needed his help with.

"There's no love lost between your mother and brother, is there?"

"You're losing me, Stefan," I say, checking my watch.

"She wanted me to punish Sebastian."

"Now that does sound like her."

"I refused, of course. He's head of your family, after all. I respect that."

"We have no head of family." It's hard to keep my irritation at his statement out of my voice. "We're not the mafia."

"Well, you understand my meaning." He's taunting me. We both fucking know it. Neither he nor I are first-born, he just got lucky, if you can call it that.

"Let's get back to why you're here."

"I'm surprised you haven't been in touch with her for so long. It's no way for a son to treat his mother. We're Italian. Family first."

"Family is complicated. You know that."

"Yeah, I do. And sometimes they fuck you, don't they?" His face hardens. "You and I have that in common," he says, studying me. "Our brothers are—or were—our rivals."

Just how much does this asshole know about me and my brother?

He finishes his drink, picks up the bottle. "May I?"

"Help yourself."

He refills his glass, sits back to watch me as he drinks.

"You know in our line of work, things are all very simple. A snitch loses his tongue, a thief, his hand. Or in this case, her sticky fingers."

Fuck.

"A traitor loses his or her life."

What the fuck did my mother do?

"Riddles, Stefan. Like I said, we're not the fucking mafia."

"I'll get to the point. Lucinda took something that belongs to me. And an act like this, after my hospitality," he says, shaking his head. "Well, I'll spare you the gruesome details, but she owes me more than I've already taken."

More than I've already taken.

"Well, you saw for yourself she's not here. My mother and I aren't close."

"She mentioned that too, but in times like this,

it's family one comes to for help. Even when that mother has turned against her own blood."

"I really can't help you, Stefan."

He swallows the rest of his whiskey, sighs.

"Amelia's lovely," he says. "You like her. I can see."

"Leave her out of this."

"I could hold on to her for you. Just until you mend bridges with your mother. While she's in town and all."

I cock my head to the side. "Are you threatening me?"

"Of course not, Gregory," he says, patting my arm. "We're old friends. I'm no threat to my friends."

"That's good because I don't take too kindly to threats." I check my watch again. "It's getting late."

"Why don't you and Amelia come by tomorrow. When it's not so late. I'm having a small party."

"We're busy."

"That's too bad. I'd love to see her again."

I'm going to fucking kill him.

He grins.

I stand.

He does the same.

He's still wearing his coat and reaches into his pocket to take out his gloves. He takes his time putting them on and there's a menace to the act.

"If you change your mind about dinner or you

happen to be in touch with your mother, I'll be at my uncle's house. You remember the address?"

I walk to the foyer.

I open the door for him to leave, but he takes his time, looking at everything as he makes his way to the foyer.

"Safe travels, Stefan. It's dangerous out there."

His expression hardens.

"What with all the ice," I add.

"I was thinking maybe she'd gone back to Philadelphia. Ethan's there, isn't he?" he asks.

I shake my head, let out a long breath.

"Go back home to Sicily, Stefan. Get a handle on your family. Maybe find your brother. Figure out who put the hit on your father. Because right now, you're not as powerful as you think. You have enemies both inside and outside your family."

His eyes turn icy, but I don't care.

"Don't fuck with me. Don't threaten me. You don't scare me," I say.

His expression remains level. I haven't ruffled him, but I didn't expect to.

"Always a pleasure dealing with the Scafoni brothers," he says, extending his hand.

I take it, but we don't shake. It's a stare down.

We were never friends, but we were also never enemies.

Tonight, that's changed.

16

AMELIA

I back away from the door as the lock turns and Gregory enters. From the look on his face, he's worried.

He comes inside, closes the door, presses the heels of his hands into his eyes.

"Fuck."

"Who is he?" I ask.

He rubs his face, looks at me. "No one."

"Well, he's someone," I say. "Matteo told me he's part of the mafia."

"Matteo talks too much." He steps closer, undoes the top buttons of my blouse and turns me so my back is to him. "Let's get a look at this."

When I draw back, he doesn't let go and I hear the tear of fabric.

"Wait."

He's walking me into the bathroom.

"Wait," I push.

He stops, impatience on his face.

"Who is he?"

"Stefan Sabbioni. And he's not *part* of the mafia. He's the head of it."

It takes me a minute to process. "What does he want with you?"

"Christ." He grips me harder, walks me backward into the bathroom, only releases me once we're inside. "Get undressed." He turns on the taps in the bath, tests the temperature of the water then dries his hands on a towel.

"I don't want a bath," I say.

"I need to think."

"What does he want?"

"Just get in the bath, Amelia." When I don't move, he takes my shoulders, gives a squeeze. It's almost tender.

Almost.

"Please get in the goddamned bath," he says through gritted teeth.

"Okay."

He nods and I think it's his thanks.

I strip off my clothes while he stands there watching me, eyes fixed on me, not quite hungry but possessive. When I'm naked, I step into the tub and sit in the warm water.

Once the tub is full, he switches off the water and takes a bar of soap out of the cabinet under the sink.

"He likes how you look."

I watch him, but it's almost like he's talking to himself and not me.

"He shouldn't have seen you. I should have hidden you."

He sits down behind me on the edge of the tub, straddling it, and rolls his sleeves up. I see ink on his right arm, just the very edges of a tattoo as muscle flexes.

"Lean forward a little," he says, setting the bar of soap down to lift my hair and adjust the clip to keep it off my neck.

His hands are strong but gentle and his fingers trace the sensitive skin at the back of my neck, and I wish I could see his face, his eyes.

When he puts a little pressure on my back, I lean farther forward.

He peels the plastic off the tattoo, and I gasp.

"I won't hurt you."

I turn my head a little, glance up, see just a corner of his face and his eyes are intent on the tattoo and I wonder if he knows what he just said, how he said it. But then his fingers are on me and it's like every nerve comes alive with just this softest touch from him.

"That fucker should know I don't share what's mine."

He's still talking to himself, not me, and growing angrier as he does.

He dips his hands into the water, turning the bar of soap between them, building a lather and I think I need to get him out of his head.

His question from earlier comes back to me, the one about ghosts.

"I see the little girl," I say out of the blue.

He stops. Looks at me.

"What girl?"

"The one who lived here before."

He doesn't seem surprised and doesn't ask questions, just begins to rub soap into my back, my shoulders and it feels so good. Different than when he touches me when we're fucking and I think it's distracting him, what I'm saying.

"I think she died that night too, with her mother. That's the dream I keep having. When you woke me that night, I was dreaming it. She wanted me to chase her into the library. She always disappears behind the shelves and I get the feeling she wants me to follow her for some reason."

That stops him. Makes him look at me oddly for a moment.

"Keep out of the library."

His tone is flat, not warning but something else. We remain still for a moment, the only sound in the room is that of the slow dripping of water into tub.

"She's not the only ghost you see," he says, and even though it's not a question, I shake my head to confirm.

"For a long time, I thought everyone saw what I saw. I realized when we were little they don't."

"How did you realize that?"

I shift my gaze away from him. I've never told anyone this.

"I asked my sisters who the girls in the library were." I can almost see them now. This image never fades.

His hands still, but they're on me and they're the only thing that's warm suddenly.

"Willow Girls," he says.

I nod.

"The shadows in the corners of your sketches," he pauses, then focuses on the work of his hands again. "Did you see the angel?"

I shake my head. "No, not like that. When I draw sometimes, it's like it's not me. Like it's not my hand moving the pencil." I turn, look up at him. "It's weird, huh? You don't believe in ghosts."

He meets my eyes. "I never said I didn't believe in ghosts. I just said they don't scare me. That the living can do more harm than the dead."

We both fall silent, listening to that dripping of water.

"I told you something, now tell me about that man," I say. "Tell me what he wants and why you're worried."

He grins, pushes a strand of hair off my face, leaves a residue of bubbles on my cheek before sliding his soapy hand down my chest to cup my breast, rub my nipple.

"Not everything is an exchange, Amelia."

He leans down, kisses me. He stretches his arm to unplug the stopper and a moment later, the water is draining from the tub and he stands me up and he's wrapping a towel around me. When I open my eyes, he's watching me with a strange look on his face.

"Ignorance can be a gift," he says.

"What?"

He snakes his hand behind my head, cradles it. He kisses me and there's an urgency to the kiss but it's not sexual. There's more to it. There's almost a texture to it, to what I taste, the feel of it.

It's a sort of need, but more.

A longing.

A loneliness that begins at the edges of it, that seeps into its heart, that takes it over and it's so much. So much that it hurts.

I open for him because it's all I can do, and I go back to what he said that time about me giving it to him. Giving him everything because he wants everything. Maybe this, me opening, it's giving that to him.

He pulls back and I can't drag my eyes from his. They're so intent on mine, like he sees me differently than anyone has seen me before and again I have to think about us, him and me, Scafoni and Willow. In a way, we're connected. Always will be. Our families have been for generations. But this, what's happening now, it's separate of that.

I'm not the Willow Girl.

I wasn't meant to be his.

I was never meant to be his.

After drying me, he lets the towel drop to the floor and leans down to kiss me again.

I'm barefoot, the top of my head barely comes to his chin and I put my hands on him, slide them beneath his shirt, feel the hard muscle of his belly, feel him pressing against his jeans and he's right. I do want more.

He draws back, looks at me, and what I want most of all is to know what he's thinking. Is to be able to read his eyes.

We walk into the bedroom and he kisses me one more time before pushing me onto the bed.

"Lie down," he says, opening a drawer, taking out a bottle of lotion and setting it on the nightstand.

I lie back.

"On your belly."

I roll onto my stomach and look over my shoulder to watch him strip off his clothes, muscles flexing as he moves.

When he's fully naked, he straddles me, knees on either side of my hips, and I draw my elbows underneath myself and look ahead as he pours lotion onto his hands, warming it before beginning to rub it into the tattoo, into my shoulders and back, lower as he shifts one knee between my legs, then the other, his hands on my ass.

I look back at him, watch him spread me open, watch the want in his eyes.

He takes his cock in his gloved hand and sets the fingers of the other on my asshole.

I make a sound, get up on my elbows, try to pull away.

"Stay," he says.

I shake my head, but he grips my hip with that gloved hand and won't let me move.

"Look at me."

He still has his finger there and I feel mortified. Again, I shake my head.

He digs his fingernails into my flesh. "I said look at me."

I crane my neck to meet his gaze and he holds mine as he pushes a finger into me and all I can do is grip the blankets as every muscle tenses.

"You need to relax," he says, moving his finger inside me, sliding his other hand around to my belly as he stretches his body alongside mine, his breath at my neck, cock hard at my back. "Do you remember what I told you?"

He's rubbing my clit and his finger inside me, it feels different than when he's touching me anywhere else.

"Amelia." He pinches my clit.

I stiffen again.

"I want everything. Do you remember that?" he asks.

I nod.

"Are you going to give it or am I going to have to take it?"

He's gentle again, rubbing my clit, moving his finger in and out of my ass and it feels good.

"Good girl," he says, feeling me relax, kissing my shoulder before pulling his finger out, rising up on his knees and lifting my hips so I'm on my elbows and knees.

His eyes meet mine as he drips more lotion onto my lower back, and he holds my gaze as he smears it inside me and when he slides his cock into my pussy, it's like I can't breathe. Like he's filled me up and all I can do is feel.

I look back at him because his face like this, he's so fucking beautiful. He looks down at me, watches his cock disappear into my pussy. He lets spit fall from his mouth down onto my ass. It's so dirty and so wrong and he's smearing spit into my ass and the thought of it, it makes me want more, more of him, all of him, but then he pulls out and I feel empty and cold, just for a single moment until he brings the head of his cock to my ass and a new panic sets in.

"Give it," he says, holding me in place. "Give it to me. Don't make me take it."

He begins to pump in slowly, stretching me, and

it hurts, but he's taking care and he's tender, in his own way, and I let myself feel his hands on me. Feel him push into me. Move inside me. Slow at first, stretching me, hurting me a little, but making it feel good, the sensations mixed up, and when he rubs my clit again, it's not long before I'm coming, before somehow, through the cloud of pain and pleasure and his fingers on me, and his cock inside me and him holding me, I'm coming and he's moving deeper and faster and it hurts again when he fucks me, really fucks me but I want it. I want to give it and I want him to take it all at once.

I tumble from orgasm to orgasm, this sensation so different than anything else, like my whole body has come alive and when I feel him swell inside me, I look back at him and I watch him, watch his beautiful face, and when he thrusts one final time, he meets my eyes and I watch him as he fills me up and all I can think is I'm his. I'm his and it's where I want to be and what I want to be, and I know it's fucked up but this is it, the truth.

He's what I want. Like this. Exactly like this.

17

GREGORY

She's tucked into the crook of my arm. I watch her as she struggles against sleep, her lashes fluttering as she opens her eyes only to have them close again. I listen to her quiet, steady breath and think how beautiful she is and how I fucked up. I should never have let Sabbioni see her. Never have let him see that she matters. Because she does.

She mumbles something, turns on her side so her back is to me. The blankets have slipped down to her waist and I can study the tattoo, the blue striking against her pale skin, the angel with her half-skull face still beautiful. The bird as if peering out from beneath the wings of the watcher, innocent. Like her.

"I could hold on to her for you. Just until you mend bridges with your mother. While she's in town and all."

I draw my arm slowly out from underneath her and slip out of the bed, pulling on my clothes and closing the bedroom door behind me.

I go downstairs to my study, sit behind my desk and pick up the phone to dial a number I never thought I'd call again.

My brother answers on the second ring.

I'm not sure what I expect to feel at the sound of his voice but as I sit here and he repeats his hello, I think I miss him. I miss my brother.

How can things get so fucked up so fast?

"Sebastian," my voice comes out more strained than I expect.

Now the pause is on his side. I hear him walking, hear a door open and close. He's probably locking himself in his study too.

"Gregory," he says after an eternity. "You're in Italy."

He can tell from my phone number. "Nowhere near the island. Don't worry."

"I wasn't worried. I heard about the house," he pauses. "You never mentioned a word about it."

He can fuck himself if he thinks I'm explaining myself.

"Stefan Sabbioni paid me a visit today."

"Sabbioni?" he sounds surprised. I guess he's not expecting this shift in conversation. What did he think? I was calling to shoot the shit? "I thought he wasn't able to leave Sicily."

"Yeah well, he did."

"What did he want with you?"

"Seems he has some business with Lucinda."

Sebastian snorts. "Lucinda. For fuck's sake she's not that stupid, is she?"

"She's still my mother, Sebastian."

"And you feel what exactly for her?"

"He's looking for her. If he finds her, things are going to get ugly."

"Fuck."

"He suggested she stole something from him."

It's silent. Sebastian knows how a thief is punished in that world.

"Do you know where she is?" I ask.

"You can't get involved, Greg."

Greg. He called me that sometimes. We used to be close. Although, I guess not that close since I didn't even tell him about the house back when I bought it, before everything happened.

"Yeah, well, I'm already involved."

"What does that mean?"

"It means he made the trip from Sicily to see me because he expects I'll deliver her to him."

"I wonder if that means his brother is no longer a threat."

Because the brother may have evidence to force the Italian authorities to extradite him. As far as I know, if Stefan Sabbioni sets foot on American soil, he'll be taken into custody and the threat is real enough that he doesn't try.

"I don't know anything about the brother. Did you know Lucinda had gone to him? After you shut her out."

"Heard something about it. Stefan wanted to be sure I knew what he did for me. I guess he thought I'd feel indebted to him."

"I want to know where she is. I need to talk to her."

"Don't get involved. It's a bad idea."

"Like I said, I'm already involved."

"How?"

I pause. "I just am. I know you're tracking her through her expenses. Are you going tell me where she is or not?"

"You're sure you know what you're doing?"

"Yes."

He sighs. "I'll send you an address."

"Thank you."

"If you need my help, you'll call—"

"I won't need your help."

There's an awkward silence. "Gregory..." he starts, but I think he changes his mind. "How are you?"

His question pisses me off more than it should. "Like you care."

I disconnect the call, put my elbows on the table, lean my head in my hands and rub my eyes.

I want it clear that I'm not asking for his friendship or approval or forgiveness or whatever the fuck he thinks he's owed. I just need to know where the fuck Lucinda is.

Within a few minutes, my phone dings with a text. An address.

In Rome.

I get up, go to the safe, open it, and take a thick stack of bills. I shove them into an envelope, get my jacket, listen at the stairs, but hear nothing. I wish Matteo were here. I don't want to leave her alone in case Stefan were to make good on his threat. But after Stefan's surprise visit, Irina was shaken and he took her to her sister's house and won't be back tonight. Everyone knows the Sabbioni family. Everyone knows to stay far, far away.

Everyone but me.

※

I park a few blocks from the hotel where Lucinda is staying and walk to the small, and very exclusive boutique hotel. I'm not sure how much of an allowance Sebastian is giving her, but this place has to be consuming most of it.

My brother's been keeping close tabs on her. Logging all of her comings and goings. Which is the only way he has this information.

But if I have it, means Stefan can get it too.

Without stopping at the front desk, I head to the elevator, giving a cursory glance around the expensively furnished lobby. As I wait for the elevator, I read the inscription on a portrait of Napoleon who apparently spent some time here.

The elevator arrives and an attendant in formal uniform steps aside for me to enter.

"Five," I say, unbuttoning my coat.

He nods, and the elevator doors close. I look straight ahead, not feeling the need to fill the silence. The elevator is old and a little rickety and I'm sure Lucinda's complained about it already.

Once on the fifth floor, I scan the hallway and turn in the direction of Lucinda's suite. At the door, I stop to listen, hearing the faint sound of the television. But when I knock, it stops.

I knock again.

"Mother," I say.

The lock turns a moment later and Lucinda stands before me. She's wearing black from head to toe and her hair is pulled back into a tight bun. Although the roots betray her age. And her state of mind.

That and the fact that she's not wearing any makeup and the buttons of her blouse are done up wrong.

I hold her gaze, although I'm curious to look down. To see if Stefan was bluffing.

"How did you find me?" she asks.

"Sebastian."

She looks at me funny. "Didn't realize you two were talking again."

"We're not."

I invite myself in and she closes the door, locks all the locks.

The room smells stale with cigarette smoke and old coffee. A room service tray from breakfast is sitting on the table by the window but the curtains are closed, and the bed is unmade.

"How long have you been in town?" I ask.

"A week."

I finally look down at the bandage on her right hand. It's a stump, only thumb and forefinger sticking out. Did he really take the others?

"Get your fill?" she asks, tucking her arm behind her back. "I can undo the bandage if you're that curious."

I don't reply but remove the shirt that's thrown over the arm of one of the two chairs at the table and sit down. I don't bother taking my coat off. I won't be staying long.

"What did you do?" I ask.

"Nothing. That boy…I knew him when he was in diapers. He's a monster, like his father."

"So, there's no reason he cut off your fingers?"

She lifts her chin, ever stubborn.

"No reason he's coming back for the rest?"

She reaches for her cup with the damaged hand, stops, uses the other one.

"Isn't that your caning hand?" I remember what she did to Helena.

"Don't forget you were once an accomplice."

"Not an accomplice." Although I was complicit. I still regret that night. I will always regret it.

She gives me a grimace, drinks a sip of old, cold coffee. "Minor detail. I'm sure it wouldn't make a difference to her if she knew."

"The only reason I didn't stop Helena from getting on that boat is because you said you were going to let her go."

She cocks her head to the side. "Come on, Gregory. Did you really believe that?"

I remain silent because did I?

"I didn't know you were going to try to kill her," I say.

"I didn't intend on killing her. Hurting her, yes. Scaring her, yes. But not killing her. Your brother was just too stupid to figure out where I'd put her."

She lights a cigarette, holds it like a joint between the thumb and forefinger of her injured hand and inhales deeply before continuing.

"Besides," she continues, blowing out smoke. "My plans only changed when Sebastian told me of his. Told me what he'd do to my son."

Ethan. She means Ethan.

She only refers to Ethan as her son. Not me. Not Sebastian.

She sits back, injured arm across her middle, watching me as ash collects on the tip of her cigarette. I wonder if she ever truly did have good intentions concerning Helena. I doubt it.

"Besides, if I had let her go, maybe you would have kidnapped her for yourself the moment my back was turned," she says.

Well, I did. Sort of.

I kidnapped a different Willow Girl.

"Guilty conscience, Gregory? All of a sudden? Because you weren't hard to convince then." She finishes the last of the drink and I wonder if it isn't laced with liquor. "Or is it because you lost the girl that you're pouting now?"

"I came to help you, Lucinda. I'm the only one still willing to help you. Remember that."

"Lucinda." She snorts. "I may not be Sebastian's mother, but I am yours." She takes a deep inhale of her cigarette, studying me. "And this help, you're doing it out of the goodness of your heart?"

I don't reply.

She smirks, like she knows the answer to that question. She gets up, goes to the cabinet, opens it and brings out a bottle of whiskey and a clean glass for me. She pours some and refills her coffee cup.

"Are you drunk?" I ask.

She swallows a big sip, looks away, and I see fear

in her eyes, and desperation. I wonder which is more dangerous.

She flicks ash off her cigarette onto the carpet then turns back to me. "Anyway, I heard you got your own Willow Girl after all."

How in hell does she know that?

I keep my face neutral but my hands fist in my lap.

"I tell you what, I don't know if those Willows have gold in their cunts or what, but you boys sure fall for them left and right, don't you? Your father did. Sebastian too. Destroyed me for his Willow whore. And now you, too?"

Her lip curls in disgust.

"The only one with any sense is Ethan," she continues. "And look what your brother did to him."

"He did it to punish you."

"Are you taking his side?" Another smirk slowly forms on her lips and I wonder how there is still so much wickedness in her. "Even now, are you taking his side?"

"There are no sides. Not with this."

"Considering everything he's done to you, you would still protect him? Considering how he and that whore have made a fool out of you *again*."

"You're talking bullshit, mother," I stand.

She reaches up, grips my arm. "Even now, they're laughing at you."

An uneasy feeling comes over me. "What are you talking about?"

That smirk grows more smug as she studies me.

"Oh, my goodness. You don't know, do you?"

I don't like the look on her face, and I want to change the subject and I want more than anything to get the hell out of here.

"Stefan Sabbioni left Sicily," I say.

"What?" That gets her attention.

"He's here."

"He can't leave Sicily. He'll be arrested."

"Yeah, well, apparently that's no longer the case. He came to see me. He's looking for you."

Now it's Lucinda who's rendered mute.

"How did you get away from him, anyway? I mean, I'd think he'd have taken all the fingers he wanted in one go." I hear the venom in my voice. I guess I'm just as wicked as my mother.

"I bribed one of the doctors who fixed this." She holds up her stump.

"Why didn't he take them all at once?"

"Because he needs me. This," she starts, holding up her bandaged hand. "This is him showing me how big his balls are."

"What does he need from you?"

She gets up, goes to the cabinet, opens it and takes out a small package wrapped up in a tissue. She brings it over to the table and sets it down, then resumes her seat.

"What is it?" I ask.

She unwraps the tissue with her damaged hand and I can't peel my eyes away from that stump. It's almost stranger for the two fingers he left.

But then I see it. The thing she took.

A ring.

I reach over, pick it up, study it.

"His brother's ring."

"Antonio?" Antonio is the rat, the brother who betrayed the family.

"It doesn't belong to Stefan. It belongs to the true head of the family."

"What business is it of yours who the head of their family is?"

"Stefan's a snot-nosed brat."

"Who cut off your fucking fingers! Are you insane?"

Her forehead wrinkles and she looks away, turns her attention to stubbing out her cigarette and I can see she's scared. Really scared.

I exhale. "Why haven't you left the country?"

"He has my passport and I'm waiting on my money from your brother to get a new one made. I tried to call him for an advance, but that prick wouldn't take my call."

"So you took a suite at one of the most expensive hotels in the city?"

She grits her teeth, her lips tightening.

I stand up, ring in my hand.

"Wait!"

"This doesn't belong to you," I say.

She knows she's in the wrong here because she doesn't counter.

I slip the ring into my pocket and take out the envelope. "This should be enough to get you a new passport. An airline ticket out of here."

She extends her hand to take it, but I pull it away.

"There's a condition."

"What condition?"

"You stay away from us. All of us. That includes Sebastian and Helena."

She cocks her head to the side, eyes narrowing, full of hatred. One corner of her mouth lifts into a cruel one-sided grin. I remember that grin from when I was little. When she scared the shit out of me.

"Don't tell me you still think you have a chance with her?" she asks.

It takes me a moment to realize she's talking about Helena. "I can also just text Stefan your location," I say with a grin that matches hers.

"You won't do that. I know you."

She's right. I won't.

But I am finished here.

I drop the envelope on the table and walk toward the door.

"It always comes down to the Willow whores for you boys, doesn't it?"

"Shut up, mother."

"You think you're so smooth. You think you have everything under control. You don't. Those Willows twist your mind..."

I open the door, wondering why I bother. Why I shouldn't let her deal with Stefan Sabbioni. She made her bed.

But I should have left before because it's when I'm out in the hallway and the door closes behind me that she does it.

That she pulls the rug out from under me.

I don't look back when I hear the door open.

"I almost forgot. Congratulations are in order," she calls out when I push the button for the elevator.

I know I should go. I know I shouldn't listen. I grit my teeth and wait. The stairs are around the corner and probably faster than the rickety old elevator.

"I hear you're going to be an uncle," she says.

It takes me a minute to process, but when I do, it's like the words have a power all their own. Sweat breaks out over my forehead and the world goes sideways for a minute, as if my brain is knocking against my skull.

Almost in slow motion, I turn on my heel, look at her.

She cocks her head to the side. "Oh. Didn't you know?"

She's enjoying this. Loving every second of it.

"Or I guess," she starts, not yet finished. "You could be the father, right? I mean it's possible, isn't it?"

Helena's pregnant?

No.

It's not possible.

"I mean, I don't know, are the brats Sebastian's or yours? Because they don't resemble either of you just yet. Look more like slithery little snakes. I have the pictures. You want to see?"

I take a step toward her.

"What are you talking about?"

"Ask her sister," she says, closing the door a little.

"What in hell are you talking about?" I roar.

Just as I reach the room, she slams the door. I pound my fist against it.

"Mother!"

The lock turns.

"Open this fucking door!"

I pound hard, hard enough other guests peer their nosy heads out of their rooms.

But I don't care because I can't think because what she's saying, it can't be.

It cannot be true.

Helena cannot be pregnant.

18

AMELIA

I'm dreaming again. I know it and I can't seem to wake myself up.

There's something different this time though. Something urgent in the way the little girl looks at me.

Her puppy is running and she's chasing her, but she keeps looking back at me and it's like she wants to be sure I'm still there, following her. She doesn't know that I can't change course even if I want to. It's like my legs are moving of their own accord.

She's hasty on the stairs and I keep calling after her to stay toward the wall. To keep away from the edge without the banister because the house, it's not like it was then. It's like it is now.

But it's not as though she can get hurt.

She's already dead.

She died the same night as her mother.

I don't know how I know this, but I do. And it's like the moment that realization dawns on me, she knows I know, too and her face shifts, is more skull-like again. No longer the pretty, carefree little girl.

A door slams and I jolt upright. Sweat drips from my forehead and I'm panting.

I look around the dark room, exhale in relief when I realize I'm still in Gregory's bed. Still here. I wasn't chasing the little girl into that library. Into whatever lies beyond that door.

A shudder runs through me and I draw in a deep, calming breath.

It's nothing. I'm still here. I woke up.

I look at Gregory's pillow, touch it. It's cold. I push the covers off get up to go into the bathroom and wash my face.

While I'm in there, I hear the bedroom door open, hear him enter.

"Where were you?" I ask as I dry my hands, feeling relieved. "You never sleep."

I hang the towel back up and turn out the light. But when I open the door to go back into the bedroom, my smile vanishes because it's not Gregory standing there. It's someone else.

"I sleep just fine," he says with a grin as if it was him I'd asked the question to.

It takes me a moment to act and I go to slam the door shut, but he's too fast and the door bounces off the toe of his boot and his giant hand curls around it as he shoves it open, propelling me backward.

I let out a scream as I look at him there, huge in the doorway in his black suit with the smell of cigarettes clinging to him.

He looks me over and I look down and I'm wearing a tiny tank top and underwear and I grab a towel as his gaze turns predatory and one side of his mouth curls upward.

"Stay away from me!" I yell, feeling for the drawer where the scissors are, my fingers slipping as I try to find the right one, try to open it.

When I manage to do that, I hear another man.

"Sorry man, had to piss," he says as he steps into the bathroom and ogles me.

I curl my fingers around the scissors, and I know I have one shot. I lunge at them, arm up, holding it like a dagger.

But they're fast and the one who just came into the room, the one closest to me jumps out of the way and I just manage to cut the other one's hand as he raises it to defend himself.

He mutters a curse and grabs hold of me, flinging me to the wall, slamming my hand against it so hard, I swear he breaks something.

The scissors clang to the floor and he closes his hand over my throat and squeezes and all I can do is try to claw his hand from me, try to suck in air. I think he's going to kill me. I think if it isn't for the other man, he'd kill me. He'd suffocate me or snap my neck and kill me.

But the other one, he puts his hand on the man's shoulder.

"Hey. Boss doesn't want her hurt."

"Fucking cunt. She cut me." He squeezes and that gurgling sound is coming from my throat.

"Calm down, man. Let her go."

He doesn't.

"Go wait downstairs. I'll bring her."

Nothing.

"I said wait downstairs." He cocks a pistol.

The man who has his hand around my throat finally releases me, and I drop to my hands and knees, panting for breath, sucking in gulps of air.

The gun is decocked and the one who strangled me mutters a curse and I think for a moment he's going to kick me, but then he's gone.

"You shouldn't have done that," the one who's still in the bathroom with me says. I look up to watch him tuck the pistol back into its holster.

He kicks the scissors across the bathroom floor, far out of reach.

"Get up," he says, taking my arm and dragging me to my feet.

"Let me go!"

He walks me calmly into the bedroom, picks up my discarded clothes from the floor. He tosses them and me onto the bed.

"Get dressed. It's cold out there."

I don't move. I just stare up at him.

"Look, if you want to go like that, I have no issue—"

"Where's Gregory?"

"Your boyfriend's not here." He looks at his watch like he's timing me.

"Where is he?" I ask more urgently.

"Time's up," he says, stepping toward me. "I guess like that it is. Let's go."

I shake my head.

He pushes his jacket back to put his hand in his pocket and I see that gun again and I think that was the point.

"Don't make me carry you. I got a bad back."

"I'm not going anywhere with you."

He shakes his head once, snorts like what I just said is funny.

"That's not up to you, sweetheart."

Next thing I know, he hauls me up by my arm and tosses me over his shoulder and mutters something about his back hurting as he carries me down the stairs, none of my fighting making any difference, like I'm a fly on the back of an elephant and he doesn't feel a thing.

When we get downstairs, the other man is waiting. He opens the door and I don't even have shoes or a coat as he takes me out into the waiting sedan, same as those I saw this afternoon, and shoves me inside and cuffs my right wrist to the handle above the door and takes his seat beside the other man as we drive away.

My heart races as the car slips on the ice, the driver taking the turns too fast. Somehow, we make it to the highway, and I recognize some of the signs. We're heading toward Rome.

I know where we're going. Who they're taking me to.

Stefan Sabbioni.

I have no doubt.

The men up front are smoking and it stinks in the car but my window is locked so I can't open it to get some fresh air. Neither of them is talking and I get the feeling they're not friends.

The one who isn't driving glances back at me after the other one says something in Italian. He nods and turns away, and about forty minute later, we take an exit and I don't think I can get any more nervous as we drive through an obviously wealthy part of town with gated properties, mansions that would dwarf the Willow house.

But the biggest house of all is on the darkest street of all.

The sedan turns onto the drive as the gates slowly inch open.

The driver rolls down his window and greets two of the soldiers standing just inside the gate and I can't look away from the machine guns they have slung over their shoulders.

But my attention is soon on the gothic mansion that comes into view at the top of the hill. Downstairs, all the lights are on, but the second floor is dark.

When we arrive at the front doors, the car stops and the man on my side opens the door. Without a word to me, he reaches in to undo my handcuff and gestures for me to step out.

I'm barefoot and in my underwear but I'd rather walk than have him carry me. The ground is icy beneath my feet and the gravel hurts, but I follow them up the half dozen steps and don't look at the guards watching me and ignore the whistle followed by another man's chuckle.

When the front door opens, I hear the soft sound of classical music accompanied by a soprano. I don't really know anything about opera to guess what it is. The large doors are closed behind us and at least it's warm in here.

I stop when the man who cuffed me tells me to wait and he talks to someone for a few minutes before gesturing for me to follow.

Marble gives way to a beautiful Persian carpet and the music grows louder as we approach the living room where I see Stefan Sabbioni sitting in front of the fire, watching it, drinking his whiskey and listening to the opera.

When I enter, the man leaves and Stefan stands. He's tall, as tall as Gregory, and built like him. He turns to me and his eyes scan me. He shakes his head and I can't think about the fact that I'm in my underwear in front of this man.

"They should have let you get dressed. You must be cold." He gestures to the seat closest to the fire.

I just stand there.

He raises an eyebrow and I realize I'm shaking and hugging my arms to myself and it's not because of the cold.

He picks up a blanket from a nearby chair and hands it to me.

"Put this around you and sit down, Amelia," he says.

He knows my name. I don't know why that upsets me. Of course, he knows my name.

I take the blanket and wrap it around myself and take the long way to the sofa to give myself more space. I perch on the edge of the couch, wrap the blanket around my shoulders and look at the fire.

"It's beautiful, isn't it? I can watch a fire all day."

I look up at him and he seems almost peaceful as he does just that, the rising crescendo of the soprano background.

But then he faces me again and even for the smile, I know there isn't anything peaceful about him. Nothing soft about this man.

"Why am I here?" I try to keep the tremor from my voice but it's impossible.

"You are perfectly safe, Amelia. You don't need to be afraid of me."

"I'm not," I lie, my voice breaking on the words.

His smile widens.

"Why am I here?" I ask again.

"Would you like something to drink?" he asks, ignoring my question and not waiting for a reply as he fills a glass for me. Whiskey from the color and smell.

I take it but have no intention of drinking it. "Why am I here?"

He sits down across from me and it takes all I have not to crumple beneath his gaze. "Incentive."

I wonder if he sees my confusion as he leans back in his seat and drinks his whiskey.

"Relax, Amelia."

I look at him. Is he serious? "You want me to relax? You kidnapped me. Your men came into the bedroom and...and..."

He shifts forward in his seat, reaches out and takes hold of my chin, raises it. He's looking at my throat which I'm sure is bruised.

"And you fought them."

"I...yes."

He shifts his gaze to mine. "They weren't to hurt you. I'm sorry they did. And I'm sorry you were afraid, but there was really no other way. You're safe now. I won't hurt you."

"Then why did you bring me here?"

He leans back in his seat. "That business is between me and Gregory. Don't worry yourself with it."

I shudder with a sudden chill.

"You must be tired."

What does he expect from me?

"Anya," he calls out, never taking his eyes off me.

A woman appears out of nowhere and I turn to her like maybe she'll help me.

Help me do what, though? Run out of here in my underwear and face the armed men at the closed gates?

"Take Amelia to her room," he says to her then turns to me.

"My room?"

"See to whatever she needs."

"But—"

"Go to bed, Amelia. We'll talk more tomorrow."

I don't move and after a moment, he gets up and comes to me and all I can think when he pulls the blanket away and takes hold of my arm to lift me up is that he lied when he said he wouldn't hurt me.

"It's time for you to go to bed."

I hate that I feel the tears building behind my eyes. That I'm so fucking afraid.

"You're tired, aren't you?" he asks.

I nod because I want to be away from him.

Stefan says one more thing in Italian to Anya that I don't catch, and when he releases me, I follow Anya up the stairs and to a bedroom where a man is standing just outside the door. He nods to her and ignores me.

I follow Anya inside and she asks me if I need anything to which I just shake my head because what I need is to get out of here and that's not on offer.

As soon as the door closes, I go to it, pull it open. I know the man will be there. It's the only reason she didn't lock me in. I meet his hard eyes and slip back inside, closing the door, taking in my new prison, a luxurious room that may as well be a cell.

19

AMELIA

There's nothing for me to do but wait and I sit beneath the blankets on the bed intending to stay awake, but at some point, I must doze off because I wake when the door is unlocked and a different woman than Anya walks into my room with a breakfast tray. The guard at my door stands waiting for her. I rub my eyes and before I can even get up or say anything, she's gone and the door is closed.

I checked the room last night and the windows were locked, and the closet empty. Although there are toiletries in the bathroom, so I brush my teeth and wash my face and return to the bedroom. I don't try the door. There's no point. Stefan is going to let me out when he wants to let me out, which is when Gregory gets here.

The coffee smells good and I pour some and

force myself to eat a bite of toast while I wait. And wait.

A few hours later—I don't know exactly because there's no clock in the room—someone comes and leaves another tray, clearing away the one from breakfast.

"Where is Stefan? Can I talk to him?" I ask her.

But she hurries along, ignoring me, pulling the door closed behind her.

I open it again but am greeted by the same man standing guard outside and I quickly step back into the bedroom, pushing it closed.

I don't eat the food this time and my hope seems to be fading with the sun. I've been here for almost a full day. He's had me locked in here for a full day.

Where was Gregory? Where had he gone after I'd fallen asleep? Does he even know I'm missing?

The next time the door opens, I'm expecting one of the girls again with another tray but when Stefan steps inside, I can't help but back up a step.

He looks me over, and I cover myself as best I can.

Anya follows him with a garment bag and some shoes as he eyes the still-full tray. "You don't like the food?"

"I'm not hungry. I want to go home."

"Home?"

I give a shake of my head. "To Gregory's house."

"I'm afraid that's not possible. Get dressed. You'll eat with me."

"I don't want to—"

He steps toward me and there's no smile and any softness I ever imagined in his eyes is gone and I wonder if it was ever there at all.

He doesn't have to say a word. He knows it. But when he reaches out to touch me, I gasp, instantly wanting to flee. But he shakes his head once and lifts my hair off my shoulder and walks around me.

"Pretty," he says, touching the tattoo, making me shudder as I wipe away tears. He turns me to face him, squeezes my shoulders. "I'm old-fashioned, though. Tattoos don't belong on a woman. Especially not one as pretty as you."

All I can do is stare up at him.

"Where's Gregory?" I ask.

"I'm sure he'll come for you the instant he realizes you're gone. I'll deal with him then. For now, I want you to go have a shower and put on that dress. Anya will help with your hair and make-up and you'll come downstairs for dinner. Am I clear?"

"Why?"

"Because I said so."

"I don't want to eat with you. I don't want to put on that dress. I don't want—"

He squeezes again, a little too hard, and leans in so his face is inches from mine. "I don't want to have to make you, Amelia."

It seems recently that all the men in my life have used that same sentence.

I try to swallow over the lump in my throat and he stands there watching me.

"Are you going to do as I say?"

I nod once.

He smiles and that dimple is back. "Good. Go get ready. I'm hungry."

Anya waits for me while I shower. She helps me put on the dress because my hands are shaking too much to do it myself. She then arranges my hair and makeup and when we're ready, she opens the door and I follow her downstairs where the music grows louder, opera again, and three men have gathered and they all look up at me as I approach.

Stefan does too and he smiles and nods in approval of the dress. It's pretty, a three-quarter length black halter dress. He's wearing a black suit with a black shirt and tie, like yesterday.

When Stefan stands, they do too. They're older, these men and the way they look at me makes my skin crawl.

"Gentlemen, if you'll excuse me." He shakes hands with each of the men who then leave together. When we're alone, Stefan turns to me. "You look very nice. He puts a hand at my back. "Let's go into my study. We'll have a drink."

I go with him because I don't know what else to

do and once we're there, he closes the door and I look around as he pours drinks.

"Whiskey okay?"

"I don't care."

He hands me one of the two glasses a moment later and smiles down at me.

"Where's Gregory? Did you hurt him?" I ask.

"I have no reason to hurt him. Not yet."

"Where is he then?"

"On his way."

I feel relieved but also anxious.

"You and Gregory have an interesting history, don't you?" he asks.

"What do you mean?"

"The Willow family and the Scafoni family. Lucinda told me a little about it and I was so curious, I did some digging myself. The Willow Girl tradition, it's archaic but so appealing all at once."

"Not to the Willow Girls, it's not."

"So Gregory lost his turn with his brother's pick and went to get his own Willow Girl, is that right?"

I don't know why this wounds me. It's true, after all. Or at least it started that way.

"You don't know anything about any of this," I say.

"No? How much do you know, Amelia? How much do you know about what happened with the Scafoni brothers and your sister? How much has he told you?"

I'm at a loss and he sees it on my face.

"I found something when I was having a look around the house. I thought you should know."

"What are you talking about?"

"Have you been to the catacombs?"

"Catacombs?"

"There's a door in the library. It'll take you there. Then you turn right. Just keep turning right until you find the room I mean. I'm curious what you'll make of what you see there. I found it very interesting," he pauses. "Honestly, I wish I could see your face when you see it."

"What are you talking about?" I ask again.

He grins, walks around me, leans in close, touches that tattoo again. "I'm happy to come and get you after you've seen that room," he whispers, trailing just his fingertips along the line of my shoulder, making the hair on the back of my neck stand on end.

I open my mouth to say something, to ask what he means when one of his men comes inside and I know from the look on Stefan's face that it's Gregory, that he's come for me.

Not a moment later, the door bursts open and he's here and two men rush in after him and grab hold of him and when Gregory gets a look at us, I think he's going to kill Stefan.

I think he's going to tear him apart with his bare hands.

20

GREGORY

"Get your goddamned hands off her!"

I'm going to kill him. I'm going to kill this mother fucker.

I didn't get back to the house until an hour ago only to find Amelia missing. Gone. Fucking vanished. And then I found that fucking invitation to the party I turned down. The asshole must have had a man outside just waiting for me to give him the opportunity to steal her away.

I haven't slept. Haven't eaten. But fuck, I drank my share of whiskey and I feel it now.

Helena is pregnant.

Helena is fucking pregnant and I find out from fucking Lucinda!

Betrayed.

Betrayed again by my brother. By Helena.

By Amelia.

Amelia.

I shift my gaze to her, and I want to strangle her and at the same time, snatch her away from Stefan.

I remember the comment about the doctor that Helena made on the phone that day, remember how Amelia pretended not to know what it was about when I questioned her. I didn't give it another thought.

Sebastian didn't say a goddamned word. Maybe that's why he was in such a hurry to get me gone. Because the baby...

They don't resemble either of you just yet.

Not baby. Babies.

They could be mine.

What if they're mine?

I shake my head, try to clear the thoughts because these last hours haven't done that. They've only intensified everything.

The image of Lucinda's bandaged hand plays before me, and I look Amelia over but she's fine. He hasn't hurt her. I don't think he intended to hurt her. He just wanted to scare me. To show me exactly how much power he has after what I said.

This is my fault.

He took her to prove a point to me.

"Gregory," Stefan says. "No need to barge in like this. I did invite you."

I tug at the men and manage to get one off balance, but a third man steps in.

"Sit down," Stefan says.

"Fuck you, Stefan."

"Are you drunk, Gregory?"

"If you don't get your hands off her—"

His grin cuts me off. That and the way he runs his fingertips along the nape of her neck.

Amelia is staring at me like she can't peel her eyes away. Like she couldn't blink if she tried. She shudders at his touch, and her knuckles are white around the glass she's holding, and I know she's terrified.

"Let her go, Stefan," I say more calmly. "She has nothing to do with this."

He steps back, looks at Amelia like he's shocked. "She's not a prisoner. We were just having a chat and a drink while waiting for you. Which by the way, it did take you a while. How's Lucinda?"

"Get your goons off me before I kill them."

"Are you going to behave?" Stefan asks me.

"Fuck you."

"There's my answer." He turns to one of his men. "Take the girl to her room while Gregory and I *talk*." He hands Amelia to the man.

She lets out a small scream when the man tugs her so hard, she almost falls.

"Let her fucking go. Don't fucking touch her!"

"You don't give the orders in my house!"

I grit my teeth, swallow my fuck you. "I have what you want," I say, stopping my struggle against the men.

He narrows his eyes at me.

"Let her go and I'll give it to you."

"Or I can just take it."

"That's not your style."

He smiles. "No, it's not." He turns to his man. "Let her go."

Amelia backs up against the far wall, eyes huge. I think in all the time I've had her, tonight is when she's truly afraid.

Stefan tucks his hands into his pockets. He gestures for his men to back off me, too.

"Come here, Amelia," I say, never taking my eyes off him.

She comes quickly and quietly to my side.

I turn to her. "Did he hurt you?"

"I'm offended," Stefan says mockingly.

I could give a fuck about him.

"Did he hurt you?" I ask her again.

She shakes her head. I think she's just barely keeping it together.

I turn to Stefan, reach into my pocket, take out his brother's ring and set it on his desk. "This is what you wanted Lucinda for. Here it is. You took her fingers. That makes you even in my book."

He looks at the ring and I don't know if he's surprised or what, but he picks it up, studies it for a long while, turning it over and over in his hand almost like he's remembering.

After an eternity, he slips it onto his finger, and I think Lucinda was wrong. I think it fits perfectly for Stefan to have the ring. To have the title of boss because he is that. His brother wasn't ever cut out for this. Stefan, though, he likes his job.

Stefan takes a sip of his whiskey and shifts his gaze to me.

"I'm afraid I'm not finished with Lucinda just yet," he informs me.

"You have what she took."

"Is that what she told you?"

Fuck.

"Thank you for returning my ring." He pours a second glass of whiskey and holds it out to me. "This business with Lucinda, you're out of it."

I don't take the glass. He sets it down, studies me.

"We're the same, you and I, you know," he says.

"We're not the same. We're nothing alike."

"On the contrary, I know something about you. I know how far you'll go to get what you want." His eyes fall on Amelia. He smiles, but when he shifts his gaze to me, that smile vanishes. "And I know what you're capable of."

He looks down at that ring again and I think what a sad victory. Top of his world and look at him.

"Let them go," he says without another glance at either of us and we're ushered out before I can say another word.

21

AMELIA

Gregory takes care with me, putting me into the car, strapping me in. Somehow, I keep it together until we drive out of those gates because I'm not sure Stefan's really going to let us go. But once we're on the road, it's like everything I felt the last twenty-four hours comes rushing out in the form of tears.

"Are you all right?" Gregory asks me once we're on the highway.

"Am I all right?" I ask, turning to him.

His jaw tightens, and his knuckles go white on the steering wheel.

"Am I all right?" I repeat. "I woke up to find you gone and those men...those men..." I wipe the back of my hand across my nose and eyes and it takes me a minute to continue. "They were inside the bedroom. I was...I wasn't even dressed. I thought it was you and it was two men and no. No, I'm not all right. I'm not even a little all right. I..."

He swerves off the road so fast that I let out a scream that's drowned out only by the angry sound of cars horns.

The tires screech as he hits the breaks and we come to a stop so fast along the side of the road that if it weren't for the seatbelt, I'm sure my face would be smashed on the dashboard.

He turns to me, takes my arms, my face.

"I'm sorry. I didn't think. I should never have left you alone. I should never have left you unprotected."

His eyes are dark and intent on me but inside them, a storm is raging. Hurt and betrayal and loss and rage. So much rage.

I reach out and touch his face and he lets me go and takes a deep breath in, pressing the back of his head into the seat and looking out into the night. A car passes too close, honks his horn.

"Fuck you!" Gregory yells at the window.

I shudder, wrap my arms around myself.

He looks at me, pulls his sweater over his head and hands it to me. "Here."

I look at it stupidly.

"Put it on. You're cold."

I take it, slide it on, look at him in his black T-shirt and think how good the wool feels, still warm from him, still smelling like him.

"He didn't hurt me. He just took me to get to

you."

"I know."

He pulls back out onto the road and I strap my seatbelt, and I think we're both a little calmer.

"What happened to you?" I ask. "Where were you?"

"I went to see my mother."

"How did you find her?"

"Sebastian."

"She took the ring from Stefan? This was all about a stupid ring?"

"Not just any ring."

I reach out, touch his shoulder because there's more. "What's going on?"

He shakes his head.

"Gregory—"

"Not now!" he snaps.

I snatch my hand away and turn back to the window and remember what Stefan said about the catacombs and remember my dream, how the girl kept trying to lead me to that door.

How did he get down there? When? That day he was at the house when we got there?

And what's down there?

Every time I glance at Gregory, I see how his forehead is creased, how he's deep in thought. And I can't help but feel outside of that thought. We're still separate. He has his secrets and I'm keeping Stefan's and it all feels wrong.

The drive to the house is long and quiet, the roads slippery once we exit the highway and head up the smaller roads to Villa de Rossi.

"Can I call my sister?" I ask once he parks the car at the house.

"What?" he asks, like he's surprised at seeing me there beside him.

"Can I have my phone to call Helena?"

He nods once and we walk in. The door's unlocked and a light is on in the living room and one upstairs in his bedroom. He left in a rush. He must have come back and found me gone and left.

"How did you know I was at Stefan's house?" I ask when we're inside.

"He left an invitation," Gregory says. "Fucking arrogant bastard."

I follow him to his study. He unlocks it, and we enter. He takes my phone out of a desk drawer and hands it to me after putting the battery in.

"You'll have to charge it," he says when it doesn't go on. He hands me a charger, I guess it's from his phone.

"Thanks."

"Listen," he says, standing there not quite looking at me, rubbing the back of his neck. He must change his mind though because he gives a shake of his head. "I need to make a call."

"Who will you call? It's late."

"Throw that dress away," is his reply.

I bite the inside of my cheek. "Okay," I say. Taking the phone and the charger, I walk out of his office, closing the door behind me.

When I hear the lock turn is when I decide what I'm going to do and I rush up to the bedroom, plug the phone in and get the flashlight I saw in the bathroom drawer alongside the scissors. I take it and go back out to the hallway, slipping off the high-heels Stefan gave me to wear and leaving them at the top of the stairs and make my way back downstairs, down through the living room and past his closed office door, to the library.

There, I switch on the flashlight and tell the voice inside my head that's screaming for me to turn around, to go back upstairs and call Helena, to shut up and I make my way to the back of the room.

I stand in front of that ancient looking wooden door for a long minute, thinking it looks like the entrance to hell. Dread fills me. I know what I'm going to find is going to be bad. I feel it. And some part of me hopes the door's locked but when I try it, I see that the lock's been broken off and I think it must have been Stefan or his men to have done that.

Does Gregory even know he went down here?

I push the door open and switch on the flashlight and shine it into the darkness before taking a deep breath in, inhaling the mix of earth and cold before stepping into the darkness.

22

AMELIA

The flashlight blinks in and out, the battery must be old, but it provides enough light that I can at least see where I'm going.

Cobwebs catch in my hair and tickle my face. I don't want to think about what's crunching under my bare feet. I wish I'd thought to put on shoes or grab a pair of socks at least.

I just follow the path and when I come to the corridor, I take the right one, like Stefan said, and I swear it's darker here and even colder.

I pass room after room without doors, and the darkness goes on forever. Like the deeper I go, the farther it stretches.

Every time I glance over my shoulder, it seems like behind me, there are a hundred ways to choose from and I think if I turned around, I'd never find my way back. Not to the library. Not back to the house.

Not back to the life I knew before the reaping.

But then finally I come to a room with a door and I know this is the one Stefan meant.

I think about what Gregory said. About ignorance being a gift. But I can't not go inside. I have to see what's here. I have to see what he's hiding.

Like the one upstairs, this door looks old and heavy, but it opens more easily than I think it will, as if the hinges have been oiled. I shine the flashlight around and in the dim light, I see candles, a lot of them on jutting stones along the walls like makeshift shelves, and sheets upon sheets of paper are stuck to the walls like posters.

But it's then that the flashlight blinks, goes out and no matter how much I slap or shake it, it won't turn back on.

I enter the room, put my hands out in front of me as I walk toward where I saw the candles. The door clicks closed behind me, making me jump, animating me to move faster. With my hands, I feel the rough, cold wall and then the smooth wax of a candle and there's a box of matches beside it, but I fumble and they drop to the floor, matchsticks scattering.

I crouch down and feel for them, blind in this solid dark, trying not to think about what I'm touching. Soon, I have the box and I light a match and it's the smallest relief in all this darkness.

My hand trembles as I bring the match to the candle, and the flame threatens to go out again when I exhale as the light takes.

I peer at the dimly illuminated sheet hanging on the wall, trying to make out what's on it. The match burns my fingertips, making me drop it and jump back.

From inside the box, I take the last match that didn't fall out, hold it to the flame of the lit candle and watch the match flare up. I light the next candle, then the one after that and the one after that and I think there must be a hundred of them. Rows and rows on the protruding stones along each of the four walls. When the match burns down, I pick up one of the candles and concentrate on lighting each one, counting as I go because what I glimpse of the pages stuck to the walls, I can't think about that. Not yet.

Some of the candles are nothing but stubs. Some brand new. And there's a box full of more shoved against one corner.

One-hundred and eight candles and the room is bathed in soft, familiar light.

Like the light in the library on the night of the reaping.

And just like that night, I turn a circle and see it repeat all around me. See that night memorialized.

Sketch after sketch, stuck one beside another, some touching, a second row of them along one wall.

Some of them are mine.

All the ones of that particular night are mine.

The missing sketchbook. Here it is. Here are all the pages of my missing book.

I walk to one of two bursts of color along these damp, black stone walls.

It's the red that marks Helena's sheath.

He must have used his finger to draw it.

Red.

Bright red.

Pig's blood. That's what they'd used to mark her dress.

I wonder if he used his own blood to mark the sketch.

Did they require my parents to use pig's blood? They could have easily used a smear of paint. Or did my mother choose to slaughter the pig? To use its blood to punish her further? Because I think she hated Helena. I just don't understand why.

My eyes fill with tears as I try to make sense of her, of my mother. I wonder if her distance from us all of our lives, if it was to prepare her for what she'd have to do.

Or what she thought she'd have to do.

The reaping.

This insane contract between our families.

All she had to do to stop it was choose us over the money, the house.

I shake my head to clear it, because that's not important anymore. It doesn't matter at all because it's done and Helena's on that island and I'm here in the middle of this room.

This memorial.

His memorial.

To her?

I remember that night when I'd had the nightmare the first time, when he woke me and I saw him, I saw how his fingers were dirty.

Charcoal.

He was using it to draw.

To modify my sketches. To draw his own. To make a monster out of himself.

I think I'm going to be sick.

It takes all I have to make my legs work, to walk slowly through the room from corner to corner, taking my time, studying each page that's stuck to the wall, touching some, tracing some of the figures.

This is what he's been hiding.

But this isn't all.

I know now why he won't let me see his back. I know what I'll find there once I do.

Two bottles of half-drunk whiskey stand on the floor beside the cot. There's a pillow and a blanket. This must be where he sleeps when he disappears at night.

I go to the bed. Sit down and pick up the pillow. I bring it to my nose, and I smell him on it, and my heart twists and I think I hate him. I want to hate him.

Because all this time, all the while that I've been here, he's only been thinking of her.

All of this has been about her.

Am I just a replica of her?

A sorry second-best?

My eyes warm with tears I despise myself for and I pick up one of the bottles and open it, pull my knees up and hug my arms around them because it's freezing down here, and I think I should have put shoes on.

I drink two gulps of whiskey.

His whiskey.

His bed.

His pillow.

His blanket.

The only thing not his is me.

Does he think I'm her?

Does he pretend I'm her when he's touching me? When he's fucking me?

Hurt turns to anger, turns to a rage that makes my blood boil and I swallow down more of the burning liquor and I can't drag my eyes from the goddamned sketches.

I sit there for an eternity just looking. Just looking all around. And when I finally get to my feet, the room spins a little. Maybe that's good though. Maybe if I pass out, I won't have to see.

I won't have to know.

"Were you in love with her?"

I suck back tears and snot and think what an idiot I am. God. What a fool. What a stupid, stupid fool.

Whiskey sloshes in the bottle, dripping over my chin, leaving its sticky sweet residue behind as some drops onto my sweater.

No.

Not mine.

His.

I put the bottle down, just for an instant, because I want the sweater off. I want it off me and I tug at the sleeves and pull it over my head and it's so cold, but I don't care.

I pick up the bottle again, drink more of the whiskey.

Being here surrounded by this, by all of this, it's like going back in time to a night I can't forget.

To the night that changed everything.

I force myself to take yet another turn, a slow circle around the room, bottle in hand. I study how he's altered my sketches, just slight modifications. Like the shadows of the ghosts of past Willow Girls who clung to the corners of the library that night— did he see them too? Feel them? Because they're more prominent now, in mine and his.

I look at the other sketches, the scenes I don't know, the ones he must have witnessed first-hand. The ones he drew.

How well he hid this from me.

How well he hid everything.

I wipe the back of my hand over my face and make myself look because it's time I see. It's past time I see.

Sebastian is holding Helena here and she's naked in his arms and I know he loves her. I can see that Sebastian loves her.

I don't want to hate my sister.

This isn't her fault.

I drink another swig of whiskey, the last of this bottle. There wasn't much in it. A quarter of the bottle? I let it drop to the floor, don't care that it shatters, don't care that I step in those shards as I make my way to the second bottle to empty that too. To drink myself into oblivion.

Her face. The detail of her face. He must have spent hours on just the details of her face.

But then I see more.

I see *them*.

And I've known all along, haven't I? Isn't it the only thing that makes any sense?

Helena and Sebastian and Gregory.

Together.

Helena between them.

Between them both.

Both brothers holding her.

Both having her.

I press my feet into the glass, wince at the pain of it cutting me. I drink.

Jealousy is hot.

Rage boils.

But betrayal, it's cold. Cold as ice.

And I'm frozen.

Betrayal makes me shudder and it makes it hard to swallow.

To breathe.

I stand before the one where Helena is in Sebastian's arms looking back, looking out of the sketch. Her eyes meet mine. I assume it was Gregory who stood where I stand now. Who watched his brother carry her away.

Watched his brother take her away from him.

I study my sister's face and the look in her eyes in this one, it's strange. Almost sorry.

I move to another and this one too, it has color. Not as bright as the red, but a deep orange. An angry, burning orange.

Helena is bound to a post, back bared, fire nearby, fire raging all around.

It's going to consume her.

It's going to consume them all.

Maybe it did.

This one, it's been ripped in two then taped back

together badly. Gregory's torn himself out then put himself back in.

I can't make out his face. He's a blur.

No, that's not true. I bring the whiskey to my mouth and drink, ignoring the cold beneath my feet, ignoring the pain of glass embedded in the skin. I study this one because as important as they all are, this one, it's haunting.

He smeared the details of his face, like he took charcoal and tried to rub it out, but I can still see it. See him.

And what I see is pain. Misery.

What I feel when I look at this is an ache so consuming, so intense and hot and burning, it hurts. It hurts like the glass under my feet. Hurts like the fire is burning my own skin.

That fire, it consumed him.

And it all finally makes sense. His fascination. His obsession.

I see clearly now for the first time since he took me. The glove too, it makes sense. I understand why he wears it, why he never takes it off.

I take that one down off the wall and resume my seat on the cot and with my finger, trace his face. And then, a minute later, I tear it, tear it right along the line where he'd torn it. I take him away from them.

And it's like that fire, that rage, it burns inside me

and I'm ripping the paper, shredding it into a hundred pieces. I let the scraps scatter along the ground and I get up and take another down, one of mine, the night of the reaping, and I do the same to that and to the next one and the one after and the one after that because I can't look at them one more time. Not for one more second.

I can't see him like this.

Can't feel him like this.

Rage bubbles over and I scream, and I don't stop tearing, ripping, destroying. I don't stop until the ground is littered with the remains of that night, the past just shreds on the floor at my feet, the walls bare.

I don't stop until the bottle is emptied and I can't walk without stumbling and when I've finished, when I'm through, I remember where I am and remember the little girl and I think is this what she wanted to show me? Is this where she was leading me to?

I want to leave.

I want to get out of here. Get out of this room. This house.

I want out.

But the door, it's flush to the wall, no doorknob, just a hole where it would be and no way to open it that I can see and when I try, I fail.

Panic overwhelms me as I scan the room again, see where I am, know that I'm trapped.

I stumble back to the cot, fall onto it when the backs of my knees hit it.

It's the liquor. It must be the liquor. I just need to think. To stay calm and think.

A deep breath reminds me of the smell of those sheaths we wore during the reaping because that rotting smell, it's here too.

Rotting earth.

He smelled like it too that night when he woke me. When I was following the little girl down here in my dream.

He'd been here.

But there's more now. Another scent. That of rotting corpses.

My mind moves to the little girl.

I lie down because all of a sudden, my head is too heavy to bear. But before I can close my eyes, before I can sleep, I have to do one more thing. One more thing to burn away that night. Burn any evidence of it. Destroy the Willow Girl Legacy.

I drop to my knees on the ground, the stones rough because this dress provides no protection. I begin to gather all the sheets of paper because ripping them apart isn't enough. They need to be destroyed and only fire can truly destroy. Can turn them to ash.

Because I think I've done what he warned me not to do.

Because I think I've fallen in love with him and I can't.

Because this...seeing this...it's not me he wants. It never was.

I never was.

Tears drop fat and heavy all around me and I don't know how there are so many to cry.

My hands and arms are dirty when I've collected most of the scraps and I see my sister's face in pieces before me. See her eyes.

I think it's the one where she's looking out as Sebastian carries her away and she's staring at me and I stare back and it's not her fault. I know that. But some part of me, it hates her.

I feel along the floor for the spilled matches. I need them. I knock over a candle in my attempt to grab the box and hot wax splashes on my arm, making me wince. The flame goes out, though, and I take care to pick up the matches and not knock the candles away.

The first strike doesn't work, neither does the second, but then, the third takes and a flame bursts in my hand and I smell the scent of sulfur and look into the flame.

I look at my sister's face, at her eyes watching me. And I drop the match into the pile of papers, and I'm surprised at how quickly the fire takes.

Almost like the pages themselves, like they wanted to burn.

To be erased from history.

From memory.

How do you burn them from skin, though?

The heat has me sitting back and an instant of terror grips me when I think what if the fire spreads? What if I can't get out?

But then there's a sound, almost like a heavy lock being lifted and the door slams against the wall and Gregory is there, and he looks at me and he looks at the fire and all the candles and I see horror on his face and all I can think is he's angry that his precious sketches are gone.

That his precious Helena is gone.

And I want to rage.

I want to scream and roar but there's a loud crashing noise behind me and as my mouth moves to form a scream, his arms are around me and he's hauling me up and pulling me back and setting me outside of the room, out of danger.

He returns inside and I sit there and hug my knees to myself as he takes the blanket and I watch him put the fire out until all that's left is black smoke and ash.

Ashes of the past.

Only memories now.

Memories are a curse. To remember is cruel.

And I can't ever seem to forget.

Gregory smells of smoke when he steps out into

the hallway and he looks at me, crouches down to touch my face.

"Are you hurt?"

I just stare back at him. "I was right, wasn't I?"

"Right?"

He looks confused but I can't think about that.

I push up on my knees and they're raw, scratched up by this unforgiving stone. I grip this shirt and I'm tearing at it, ripping it apart, but it doesn't give, not right away.

But he's still and he lets me.

He lets me open it, push it off his shoulders, lets it hang halfway down his arms and I touch them, look at my hands on him—so small around powerful muscle, so pale against all that ink.

I get up and I walk around him, and I'm coughing from the smoke and the smell of rot and I look at his back, at the chaos of tattoos there, image upon image carved into his skin.

"Amelia." His voice is low, quiet and calm.

"No!" Mine is the opposite.

I pound my fist into his shoulder.

"I hate you. I hate you."

"Stop, Amelia." But he doesn't move to stop me and he's on his knees at my feet and I'm beating my fists into him and he's letting me. He's just letting me.

I hit him again and again. Harder. I want to

scratch away his skin, rip it away, dig away the past with my fingernails.

I want to make him hurt.

I want to make him bleed.

And that sound, that of a mad woman, it's me. It's my screams.

He stands up finally, finally. He turns, takes my wrists and walks me backward, presses me into the wall.

"No!" I yell again, fighting him. Wrestling against him but wanting him. Needing him.

Needing to hate him.

Needing him to want me.

"Stop!"

His eyes are dark, and he looks me over and in the next instant, he's pressing his mouth to mine and he's kissing me and the back of my head hurts from the stone, but he won't let up and so I bite. I bite him hard and I want it to hurt and all I taste is the metallic taste of his blood and the salt of my tears and this is what we'll have.

This is for us. For him and me.

Blood and tears and pain and hate.

"I'm not her," I yell when he pulls back a little, his breathing short, ragged, my fight draining, leaving my limbs heavy, seating a brick inside my belly. "I'm not her."

He watches me, fingers hurting my face when I try to turn away.

"I'm not her." I'm crying. Sobbing. "I'm not. I won't ever be her."

He's tearing at my dress, ripping it. He's hurried and his hands are rough, and the stone is shredding the skin of my back.

"I don't want her," he says finally. "I don't want her."

I dig my nails into his face, and he doesn't stop me. Just keeps ripping at my clothes.

"I love you, Amelia. You."

I don't hear him. I can't. "I'm not her." It's like a mantra. Like a never-ending chant. "I'm not her."

"You stupid, stupid girl. It's *you*. You're for me."

Skin collects beneath my nails and he presses his body against mine, trapping me between him and the wall and undoing his jeans, shifting his grip to my hips, lifting me higher only to impale me on his cock, thick and ready and painful, painful enough to make me scream.

He looks at me when I do and thrusts again and I know he won't stop, and I don't want him to.

I want him. I want him like this.

And I hate him at the same time. I hate him for having wanted her.

When he kisses me, the blood on his lips smears my mouth, my face and when he fucks me, it's hard and he's hurting me, and I'm clinging to him and his eyes, it's like they see inside me and I think he's going to split me in two because he can't get close enough either. He can't get close enough.

And all I can think is how beautiful he is. Even now. Even like this. How very fucking beautiful like that angel inked into my back.

Breaking.

Broken.

Beautiful.

A broken monster and an angel in one.

23

GREGORY

I push the image of what I saw behind the crumbling stone wall from my mind. I'll deal with that later.

My shirt is hanging from my shoulders, Amelia's dress is a rag. And we both stink of that room and smoke and fire and I think I never want to go back there again. I never want to go back underground again.

I pull out of her, set her down.

Her hands fall off my shoulders and when I stand back, I watch her slide to the floor, watch her bring dirty hands to her face, wipe away a tear only to leave a smear of dirt on her temple.

When she looks up at me, her eyes, the look inside them, it breaks me a little.

I thought that night, the night of the branding, I thought that broke me. But I was wrong because this, the way she looks at me now, this is what breaks me.

"Amelia."

She puts a hand on the ground, tries to push up to stand and when she stumbles, almost falling back down, I catch her and when she shoves at me, I smell whiskey and fire.

"How much did you drink?" I ask when I have her up on her feet. If I let her go, she'll fall.

She slaps her hands flat on my chest and I see the effort it takes her to straighten.

"I'm not her," she says again.

When she tries to shove me away, I take hold of her wrists and pull her arms to her sides then behind her to hold them in one of mine as I grip the hair at the back of her head with my other hand and force her head backward.

"Hear me, Amelia," I say, pulling her closer so my nose is almost touching hers. "I don't want her."

"I'm not—"

"I. Don't. Want. Her."

The rage in her eyes gives way to hurt and my heart twists to see it and she should never have been down here. Never have seen that room.

I should have destroyed all of those sketches long ago. I should have set them on fire myself.

I soften my grip in her hair and she drops the top of her head into my chest and I hear her cry and feel the wet warmth of tears and I'm so fucking finished with tears. So fucking finished with the past.

I bow my head, set my lips on top of hers. I kiss her and I don't think she hears my whisper. I know she doesn't.

When I started this, it was about Helena.

When I decided this, it was because I didn't get the girl.

Because I wanted to punish Helena.

But it's different now. Everything is different. It's been different ever since I first walked into that apartment and saw those sketches and inside them, I saw her. I saw Amelia.

I wrap my arms around her and she's freezing.

"It's you, Amelia. You." I push hair from her face. "You're for me."

She doesn't fight me when I lift her up, but she does turn her face away, hides it in the crook of my neck.

I want her out of here. Out of this cold. This dark.

I carry her to my room, to my bed. I lay her down and take off the rags of her dress. I clean the cuts on her feet from the broken bottle of whiskey and when I'm done, I lie beside her, and I kiss her cheeks, her temples, her eyelids. Take her hand in mine and feel how soft she is, and I've never wanted to be this close to anyone before. No, it's not that. It's not a want.

"It was me," I say.

She looks at me, and I think how tired she must be. How utterly drained.

"Charlie. Liona. The apartment. It was all me. I hired them. I paid them. I set it all up. It was all me from the very beginning."

She turns away, but I touch her face, make her look at me.

"I could have just taken you, like I did anyway, but I wanted the game. I wanted to fuck with you. And you were right. It was all to hurt her."

Her forehead wrinkles and I think about everything she would have seen down there. All those scenes from the island.

Sebastian. Helena. Me.

"Stop," she says weakly, trying again to look away.

I shake my head.

"But then I saw the drawings," I say. "Everything changed when I saw that sketchbook. Every single thing."

Her sad eyes study me.

"And then I watched you all those nights. I saw your face. And what I saw, you were like this..." I search for the words and wipe away the tears sliding down her cheeks and I see my gloved hand, and I think how strange it is, how that glove doesn't belong.

Not anymore.

"You were like this strange, beautiful, broken

thing. You were in pieces. And all that time, what I wanted, what I was doing, was collecting all those pieces of you and I didn't even know it."

She takes my hand in hers and I can see in her eyes what she would have seen down in that room and I feel it again, that angry fire.

When she begins to peel off the glove, I don't stop her.

She sets the glove aside.

I don't know what I expect she'll do when she sees it. Jump. Scream. Be repulsed.

But she does none of those things. Instead, she touches the scarred, raw skin of my hand. Traces the deep crescent-shaped wedge burned out of my palm.

"You stopped him from branding her."

I snort. "I'm not the hero and my brother isn't the monster. It was because of me it would have happened at all. I only stopped what I started."

"Did you love her?"

I lean my head against the headboard and study the ceiling for a long time before looking back at her.

"I need you to answer that."

She deserves an answer to this question. I know it. "What happened on that island had nothing to do with love. Not where I was concerned."

Sadness, only sadness.

"Did you hear what I said to you?" I ask.

"What?"

"Downstairs. In the catacombs."

"You said you don't want her."

"What else?"

Her gaze shifts to her lap, thick lashes hiding her eyes from me.

"What else, Amelia?"

It takes her an eternity to look up at me. "You said that you love me."

24

AMELIA

I watch him watch me.

He touches my face, leans toward me, kisses my mouth.

I close my eyes, and he's so gentle, so soft with me.

I put my hand on his chest and I kiss him back and it's like we're doing it for the first time. Like this, like it's the first time we touch. First time we kiss.

"I love you," he says against my mouth.

I slide my fingers into his hair as he rolls me onto my back and lies on top of me and I like his weight on me. It feels safe and for some reason, I find myself crying again and he's kissing me harder and I think about what he warned me not to do that first day. When he told me not to fall in love with him.

I think I've loved him for a long time. Long before he brought me to this house.

He draws back, looks at my tears.

I shake my head, pull him to me. We smell like smoke and earth, but I don't care.

I kiss him again, wrap one leg around his middle and when he slides inside me, he looks at me again, like he likes watching me take him.

"Why?" I ask.

"Why what?" He stops moving, pushes dark hair from my face, his fingers soft and warm on my skin, warmer than that leather.

"Why do you love me?"

He smiles. It's the softest smile I've ever seen. "Because I'm in pieces too and only when I'm inside you am I whole."

He moves inside me and he's warm and big and I feel safe, feel like he'll never let me go and I cling to him because how he feels, it's how I feel too.

I think I needed him to take me like he did. I think there wasn't ever anything else for me. Never anyone else.

He draws up a little, watching me as his thrusts go deeper, faster, harder, and he looks at me like he does, I arch my back and I lean up to kiss him, eyes open, to lick his cut lip and kiss him and feel him thicken inside me and we come together, connected in every way, and I think I can't ever be without him. I can't ever be away from this man. Because those pieces he's collected, he's still got them, and I don't want them back because I won't ever be whole without him.

But as the orgasm passes and we lie panting together, the heavy weight of reality returns.

"I need to tell you something," I say.

He rolls onto his back, looks up at the ceiling.

"Helena's pregnant."

His reaction is different than I expect, and he nods slowly and the look in his eyes, it's strange, almost resigned.

"You knew?" I ask.

"I found out the other night," he says, shifting his gaze to me.

"How?"

"My mother."

"How did she know?"

"It doesn't matter, not anymore. None of it does."

I have to say this next part. I don't want to. God knows, I don't want to, but I have to. And I know he's thought about it too.

"You could be the father."

As if on cue, my phone that's charging beside the bed, buzzes. I look at it, watch it vibrate along the nightstand. It's face-down so I don't see who it is. I reach for it but I'm too late and the screen shows the missed call.

All of the missed calls.

I sit up and scroll through them. Scroll through call after call.

Sebastian.

They're all from him.

There must be twenty attempts in the last twenty-four hours.

I push my hair behind my ear. "Something's wrong."

Before I can call him back, it vibrates in my hand. It's Sebastian again.

I swipe to answer. "Hello?"

I'm right. Something's wrong. I can hear it in the way he breathes. Feel it in the weight of silence.

"Where have you been?" His voice is strained, hoarse, like he can just manage to get the words out.

"What's happened?" I'm already crying.

"She tried to call you. I fucking tried—" His voice breaks.

"Where's my sister?" I ask, suddenly frantic. "Where's Helena?"

"You need to come."

"Where's Helena?" I scream.

"The babies." He stops like he can't go on and silence seeps into the emptiness.

The babies?

"What?" I finally ask, my voice barely above a whisper.

He doesn't need to say it though. I know. I already know.

"It's too soon. One..."

25

GREGORY

"But...it's too early," Amelia says.

I take the phone from her, push the speaker button.

"It was too much for Helena. She was too small to carry four—" I hear my brother's voice break.

Hear *him* break.

I thought I would enjoy that sound. That it would give me pleasure.

A new panic takes hold of Amelia. I see it on her white face. "Where's my sister?"

"She's in the hospital. They all are."

"Is she okay?"

"She will be, physically," he pauses. "You need to come now. She needs you to come."

Amelia just nods, relieved but like she's still processing.

"Get to the airport. Get on the next flight out. I'll send money."

Amelia's eyes meet mine.

I clear my throat, take the phone off speaker and set it to my ear. "I'll bring her."

Silence, then: "Gregory?"

"Let me know which hospital. I'll bring her."

I wait. It's his turn to process now. "What in hell—"

"We can do battle when I get there, brother. Send me the address." I hang up the phone, get off the bed. "Go shower, I'll pack some things," I tell Amelia.

"But—"

"It's about a four-hour drive to Venice. We'll be there by morning if we hurry." She opens her mouth to speak, but I cut her off. "Go."

The drive to Venice is a tense one. Amelia is worried about her sister. She's worried about the babies. And I'm sure she's worried about what Helena will say when she sees her with me.

Me, I could give a fuck what Sebastian or Helena think as far as Amelia and I go. And Sebastian and I, we have some talking to do. But I've never heard him sound like he did on the phone just now.

Amelia's phone vibrates with a text message when we're about half an hour from the hospital.

"He wants me to text him when we get there. Says it'll be best if I go in alone."

I turn off the highway, glance at her. "What do you want?"

"I don't want to shock my sister. I mean," she touches her hair, which she's been wearing parted on the side to cover up the handful I cut off. "I already look very different."

I nod, although I'm not sure how I feel about it. I won't hide from them.

An icy rain is falling by the time we arrive at the hospital, my brother is waiting just inside the entrance. He comes outside as soon as I pull up to the curb.

Amelia opens the door and climbs out, stops.

I realize this is the first time she's seen him since the reaping.

After killing the engine, I get out, meet his eyes as he stalks toward us. I get to Amelia just as he does and step half way between them.

"Brother," I say.

"I'll deal with you later," he says to me. He turns to Amelia. He takes in her shorter, dark hair. "You'll explain everything to me first. Not a word to Helena. I don't want her upset, understand?"

She nods.

I roll my eyes, shake my head, give a snort.

"I'll take you up to see her," Sebastian says, ignoring me.

"How is she?" Amelia asks.

"Scared mostly. Sad."

"Are the babies..."

"Incubated." His forehead furrows. "They're so small. And one...she's...the doctor isn't sure—" his voice breaks.

"What happened?" I ask.

He looks at me, almost doesn't answer, but Amelia asks the same question.

"Helena started to cramp badly. It had been happening for days, but you know how she is. Just dismissed it. Didn't want to make something out of nothing." He shakes his head. "By the time we got here, she'd lost a lot of blood. Almost went into hypovolemic shock. They took her into surgery right away. She didn't even know until afterwards what had happened. Didn't know that they took the babies."

"God," Amelia's voice is a whisper.

"She almost didn't..."

My brother's eyes are bloodshot, his hair disheveled. There are dark red stains on the cuffs of his shirt that I don't think he's aware of.

"Let's go," Sebastian says.

"I'll park the car," I say. Amelia hesitates, turns to me. "I'll see you in a few minutes," I tell her.

"You'll wait in the lobby," Sebastian says to me as I'm getting back into the car.

I'll let it go, considering.

In the rearview mirror, I watch Amelia and

Sebastian disappear into the hospital. I find a parking spot and head back to the entrance a few minutes later, entering just as the elevator doors open and my brother steps out to greet me.

26

AMELIA

I've never seen Helena look as frail as she does lying in that hospital bed. I've never seen her look as sad.

But when I walk inside, she sits up, wincing, and I can tell she's in pain.

"Amy." My name sounds like an exhale.

I smile, rush to her and wrap my arms around her. I missed my sister. I missed her so much more than I realized, and I don't know how I could ever have thought that I hated her.

"Helena, I'm so sorry." For so many things.

She hugs me tight and just holds me like that for a long time and I hear her cry and I just hold her back.

"I'm so sorry," I repeat as she releases me, leans back in the bed looking at me, taking in my new hair color. I don't want to talk about that yet, though. "How are my nieces?"

She smiles at that and I pull a chair up to the bed to sit.

"I think they'd fit in the palms of Sebastian's hands," she says.

"That small."

"We knew they'd be small, but this is too early. One of them, the doctor isn't sure she's going to make it."

"No, don't say that. She's alive. They all are. You are. That's what matters."

God. My sister. If something had happened to her, I don't know what I'd do.

She nods, and I can see her steeling herself. "Your hair," she finally says.

I touch it, look at the dark strands. I think it's time to go back to my natural color. This isn't me. Not anymore.

I consider lying to her about it. Telling her it was for a shoot. But the idea of weaving another story, it's exhausting.

"I wanted something different," I say.

She studies me, and I wonder what she sees.

"Amy, where have you been? We've been calling you for days."

What do I tell her? That I've been lying to her? That Gregory Scafoni kidnapped me? That I'm in love with him?

I open my mouth to answer, not sure what I'm going to say, not wanting to upset her, not now.

"Where are the babies?" I ask instead.

"NICU."

"Do they have names yet?"

She's studying me, her eyes intense. "Samantha, for Sebastian's mother, Libby, Charlotte, just because I like that name, and the littlest one, she's Helena. For Aunt Helena," she clarifies.

"Then she's strong." I feel my eyes water. "All Helena's are strong."

"You look different, Amy."

I just watch her.

"What's happened to you?"

I look down at my lap, wipe a lone tear.

"Where have you been?" she asks.

Just then the door opens and a nurse walks in, smiling wide and carrying a tray of food. "Time for breakfast," she says to Helena, then turns to me, gives me a warm greeting. "Is this your sister? I can see the resemblance."

"I'm Amelia," I say, grateful for the interruption as I get to my feet and push the chair back to make room for her to set the tray down.

"I'm not hungry," Helena says.

"But you need to eat. Those girls need you to be strong now."

I think Helena's going to burst into tears again.

A doctor walks in flipping through a chart.

"Good morning, Helena," he says. "How are you feeling this morning?"

The nurse turns to me. "The doctor just needs a few minutes. Would you like some coffee?"

"I'd love some." I give Helena's hand a squeeze before slipping away. "I saw a café down in the lobby," I say, quickly heading to the elevator, disappearing into it before she can say anything.

27

GREGORY

"When were you going to tell me?" I ask my brother.

"They're not yours," he says flat out.

I don't know what I expect to feel at that, but I don't feel anything at all.

"We had tests run early on. I'm the father," he adds.

"Well, congratulations."

"Don't be a dick, Gregory."

I shut my mouth. He's right. Now's not the time.

"How is she?" I ask, my tone somber.

"She'll be okay. If we'd been a little later, she wouldn't have been."

I nod, because this, I do feel something. Relief. "And the babies?"

"It's still early. She was only twenty-six weeks

pregnant and three are stronger than the one. First one."

"Will they be okay?"

"The three have a better chance, but they're all fighters. Like their mother."

"And their father." I give him that and we study each other for a long minute.

"Why is Amelia Willow with you?" he finally asks.

Of course, he was going to ask that.

"Interesting story, that," I start with a chuckle, and I realize it's badly timed, but there wasn't ever going to be a good time to tell this particular story so, when Sebastian grabs me by the collar of my shirt and shoves me backward into the wall, I'm not surprised.

But I am pissed.

I grab him back, shove him into the other wall. "I guess you were right. I wanted my own Willow Girl."

We turn a slow circle in the lobby, hands fisted at each other's throats, the way we always seem to end up when the conversation turns to the Willow Girls.

"If you hurt that girl—"

"What? You think you're the only one entitled to one?"

"There's only one, you know that. The rules—"

"Yeah, well, I guess I don't play by those rules anymore."

"What did you do to her?"

"I didn't have to do anything *to* her, brother. I guess that's where we differ."

The elevator dings and Amelia steps out, gasps. I imagine how we must look to her. Like we're about to kill each other.

"What are you doing?" she yells.

Neither Sebastian nor I break eye contact or reply.

"Are you crazy? Let go of each other!" Amelia is beside us, a hand on each of us trying to shove us apart, and I remember this same scenario a few months back, us in Joseph Gallo's office. It was Helena trying to pry us apart then.

"Did he hurt you?" Sebastian asks Amelia but keeps his eyes on me.

I snort.

He tightens his fist and I tighten mine in response.

"If he made you do anything…if he hurt you in any way, know that I will kill him," he says more to me than to her.

"My brother, always the white knight. You don't know the half of it, Amelia. Tell me something, Sebastian. Is the pregnancy the reason you were in such a hurry to get rid of me? Why you didn't fight my demands?"

"I already told you, I'm the father, not you."

"Stop it. Both of you. Stop," Amelia interjects.

"I'm sure you didn't know that fast," I say.

"Go back upstairs, Amelia. I'll be there in a minute," Sebastian says sounding calmer than I feel. But him telling Amelia what to do, like she's his, it gets under my skin like nothing else.

"You don't get to tell her what to do." It comes out a snarl.

"I'm not going anywhere until you let go of each other," Amelia says. "You're both being crazy!"

Sebastian finally turns to her, looks her over. His gaze falls to her dark hair and when he returns his narrowed eyes to me, I can just imagine what he's thinking.

"I'm going to kill you," Sebastian says, shoving me into the wall. "I'm going to fucking kill you."

"Stop!" Amelia sets herself between us just as Sebastian readies to swing.

"Amelia!" I shove her away because she's going to get hurt, and in that instant of distraction, Sebastian's fist collides with my face and for a moment, everything goes black and I stumble.

Amelia screams.

I give my head a shake, straighten, lunge for my brother, my fist in his gut making him double over with a grunt.

"It's not what you think," Amelia yells. "Stop!"

But before either of us can land another hit, four security guards show up, two for each of us, taking us by the arms and dragging us out into the icy rain.

They're yelling something but I can't hear them, and I don't think Sebastian can either.

"Did you pretend she was Helena? You sick bastard!"

The guards hold him back and I see Amelia follow us out and I hope she didn't hear that, but I think she did.

"She did that herself, prick. She dyed her hair before I even got hold of her."

"Got hold of her? What did you do, stalk her? Kidnap her?"

"Is it any different than what you did?"

"I had no choice and you know it!"

"You had every choice, and so did I and you know the difference between me and you, brother? I own it. I fucking own my choices." I shrug at the hands on my arms. "Get off me!" But they don't let me go.

Amelia is standing at the entrance, icy rain soaking her.

It's soaking all of us.

"I'm done," I say to the men, stopping my struggle. "Finished."

They let me go. I turn to her, then look back at my brother. "I did want Helena. Before. That's finished too. It finished that night in Lucinda's house. And I'm sorry for what's happened to her. To both of you. To those babies."

I go to Amelia, look at her tear and rain-soaked face. I touch her cheek, feel the icy cold skin.

"But I'm not sorry for taking her," I say to Sebastian but look at Amelia. "And I'm not giving you up." The last part I say only to her because fuck my brother. I owe him nothing.

I wrap my hand around Amelia's arm and turn to Sebastian whom the guards have released.

He stands looks from me to Amelia and I think one word from her, and he'll kill me. But she leans her body into mine, slides her free hand into my damaged one.

"I love you," she says, and I hold her closer and I'm not giving her up and no one's taking her from me. I'll kill anyone who tries.

Sebastian rubs his eyes, his face. "Fuck."

Amelia's teeth chatter.

"It's cold," he says. "Get her inside."

28

GREGORY

It's afternoon before Sebastian comes back to the lobby, to the café where Amelia and I are waiting. He doesn't say much, just gestures for us to follow.

The elevator ride is tense, none of us speaking. I'm not sure what to expect as we step off the elevator and head together to Helena's room, but Amelia's hand is sweaty in mine. She's nervous.

Sebastian enters first, stands at the head of the bed beside Helena who looks at Amelia like she's betrayed her. But then her gaze falls on me and that look, it's different. Almost violent.

I study her. It's the first time I'm seeing her in months. She's pale and I can see she's uncomfortable, but still, in spite of everything, she's Helena. She's beautiful and strong. And she still hates me.

"Helena," Amelia starts.

"No," Helena interrupts, her gaze just slipping to mine for an instant before returning to her sister. "No, Amy."

Sebastian's hand is on Helena's shoulder, squeezing just a little and I wonder how he told her. What he told her.

"She's innocent," Helena says to me.

I raise my eyebrows.

"And you're a bastard."

"What are you, then?" I ask because fuck this double standard. Fuck it.

"Watch it," Sebastian warns.

I look at my brother's face and I see the same thing I saw every day on that island, and I don't know how I didn't understand it then. He loves her fiercely. He will protect her fiercely even against me.

And I guess that's how it should be.

"You should have left her alone, Gregory. It's not right," Helena says.

"Don't I get a say in this?" Amelia asks.

"You're not to blame—" Helena starts.

"I love him," Amelia blurts, cutting her off. Helena shifts her gaze to her sister, and it softens instantly. "And I don't need you to protect me, Helena. Not anymore."

"How? How can you love him?" Helena asks.

"Am I that terrible?" I interject with a snort.

"You shut up," Sebastian says to me, eyes narrowed.

Helena ignores us both. "How can you love *him*?"

The way she says it, the *him*, she's almost spitting the word.

I feel Amelia straighten beside me. She's steeling her spine. She slips her hand from mine.

"Same way you can love him," she says, gesturing to Sebastian. "There's nothing different. The way it started for us, it's the same way it started with you. And then something happened. Just like it did for you."

Amelia walks to the bed, sits on the edge of it. I see the tears that fill Helena's eyes as she slips her hand over her sister's.

"When we grew up, there were two sets of rules," Amelia starts. "One for you and one for the rest of us. It wasn't fair to you then and it's not fair to me now."

"We were kids. That was different, Amy. There's too much that's happened, things you can't know."

"But I do know, Helena."

Helena stares back at her, not quite believing her, I guess.

"I know what happened," Amelia continues. "I know everything. He told me everything."

"Are you sure?" I can see that Helena's torn. I know she doesn't want to hurt her sister.

"Yeah. I am. I know. I know about you, and him and them."

Helena's gaze slips from her sister's, slides to me for a moment.

"I know all of it, and it doesn't matter. Not anymore." Amelia wipes the back of her hand across her nose, stands. "Please don't make me choose, Helena. I don't want to lose you."

Helena watches her, and I watch the tear slide down Helena's cheek and I remember that time on the island and I think again how fast things change. How love—no—how indifference can turn to hate so quickly. In the blink of an eye.

Sebastian leans down, whispers something to her.

She shakes her head, looks away.

He whispers it again, kisses her cheek.

"I know," she says. She looks back at us. "I want to talk to Gregory alone."

"I don't think that's a good idea," Sebastian says, as Amelia takes a step toward me.

"Please just wait outside. Both of you."

Sebastian straightens, gives me a warning look. "Don't upset her," he tells me as he passes.

Amelia reluctantly follows Sebastian out. When the door closes, Helena looks at me.

"What?" I ask, raising my eyebrows, not feeling the hate I want to feel.

"She's young."

"She's the same age as you."

"You know what I mean."

"She's not as naïve as you think. And she knows what she wants."

"And she wants you?"

"Is that so hard to believe? Am I that much a monster?"

She lowers her lashes and I'm not sure if her gaze falls on my hand by accident or not, but she gasps when she sees it.

I shove it into my pocket pissed at myself for caring.

When she returns her gaze to mine, it's different how she looks at me.

She holds out her hand.

I stay put.

"Please," she says.

"What do you want, Helena?"

She shifts, winces as she pulls herself up a little.

Crap.

"Are they giving you something for the pain?" I ask. I don't want to care.

She nods. "It's fine. I'm fine." She looks back up at me. "I heard you, you know."

The tears collected inside her eyes spill down her cheeks and she wipes them away with the back of her hand and all I can do is stand there and watch her.

"The night of the branding. I heard you."

I pull my hand out of my pocket, rub the back of my neck, look away from her.

"Well, I was sorry too," she says. "I *am* sorry. What we did, it was wrong. I knew it but I went along with it and it was selfish and I'm sorry, Gregory. I'm sorry we hurt you."

I meet her eyes.

I hadn't thought she'd heard when I'd whispered my apology. I'd thought she was passed out.

She's waiting for me to say something, but I simply nod my head. She moves again, clutches her belly this time.

I reach for the remote to push the call button, but she pulls it away.

"I'm fine."

"You're not fine."

"My sister—"

"I love her, Helena. I'm not going to hurt her. But I'm not asking for your blessing. Neither of us are. I do know, however, how much it would hurt her to lose you again. Just know that I love her. That it's real with her."

She studies me for a long time and finally extends her hand again. "Let me see your hand."

I sit on the edge of the bed, hold it out.

She traces the pattern burned inside it and there was a time I would have felt something at her touch, but that time is past. She looks up at me.

"You saved me from this."

"I put you in that position in the first place."

She's quiet for a long minute.

"Did you see the girls?" she asks.

I smile. This is her acceptance. Her apology. Her forgiveness.

Mine too, maybe.

"My nieces?"

She nods.

"Not yet."

"Sebastian should take you," she says, but her smile is pitiful.

I shift my hand so I'm holding hers and squeeze. "They'll survive, Helena. I have no doubt."

And I don't.

29

AMELIA

Six months later.

They do survive, all of them.

And for all the generations of blonde-haired Willow daughters, they all resemble Helena, but only the littlest has the silver streak in her hair.

"She's tough, this one," I say, handing her back to Helena.

We're standing on the dock, Gregory and I readying to leave. The sun is hot and bright and the water of the Adriatic glistens all around the island. It's a magical place, this. But it's not home.

"Can't you stay?" Helena asks again.

"It's past time I picked up my life and figured out what I'm doing with it."

I've been with Helena on the island since she was released from the hospital. Gregory's been back and forth from Rome managing the final stages of construction on the house.

"I'm going to miss you," Helena says.

"Me too."

We turn to watch Sebastian and Gregory walking toward us, Gregory carrying our bags, Sebastian holding another one of the quadruplets.

It took a few weeks for Sebastian and Helena to fully accept that Gregory and I were together, but they did, and the brothers patched things up. I'm glad for it because as much as Gregory would never admit to feeling hurt or missing his brother, I know he did.

"She was fussing," Sebastian says to Helena about the baby. "I didn't want her to wake the other two."

"Ready?" Gregory asks.

I nod. As much as I'll miss my sister, I am looking forward to the next chapter of my life. I feel like it's the first one where I'm in control of it. Of myself. My destiny.

Helena hands the baby to Sebastian who still looks strange holding the tiny little things, although he's a great dad and takes wonderful care of Helena. She wraps her arms around me, and I hug her back.

"Christmas in Rome," I say. "We'll have a full month together."

Helena squeezes me. "I can't wait." She pulls back and we watch Gregory loading the bags onto the boat. "You're good for him," she says.

I just nod, not taking my eyes off him.

She turns to me, touches my blonde hair. "And I like this better on you." I dyed it back to my natural color shortly after our reunion.

"Me too."

Gregory returns and Helena smiles. "You better take good care of my sister," she says to him, and although it's meant to be a joke, I know there's seriousness too.

"You take good care of my nieces," he tells her.

"You spoiled them." He does. Gregory is better with babies than I guessed he would be.

"It's my job," he says.

"If you need anything—" Sebastian starts to say to me.

"Christ," Gregory cuts him off, wraps an arm around me. "If she needs anything, I'll take care of it."

Helena takes both babies and Gregory and Sebastian shake hands, then hug like men hug, with a quick pat on the back. "See you in a few months, brother."

Gregory nods. "See you in a few months."

We get on the boat and Remy drives away, the engine loud, the breeze not quite cool. When they're just dots in the distance, Gregory wraps his hand around mine.

"Okay?" he asks.

I turn to him. "Yeah." I push wind-blown hair back from his face. "Yeah, I'm good."

He wraps his arm around my waist and pulls me closer and the way he looks at me sometimes, it's like he still can't believe it's real because I know I can't. Where we came from, where we started, it's the strangest thing. The most impossible thing.

"I love you," he says.

He leans down and kisses me, and I wrap my hands around the back of his neck and kiss him back and when we break the kiss, I lean my cheek into his chest and close my eyes.

"I love you too."

30
GREGORY

*A*melia hasn't seen the house in six months. The sun is setting as we approach it and I realize it's the first time she's seeing it after the thaw of snow.

This winter was harsh with more snowfall and ice than the city's seen in a hundred years. It fits, in a way. For a long time, it felt like she and I were frozen in time. Like neither of us could get beyond what happened.

I push the button to open the gates and she sits up, looking anxiously ahead, looking every which way, taking in the lush green gardens, the water flowing from the fountain which was once just crumbling rock.

I park the car and we climb out and I look at her and smile.

"Wow," she manages when I go to her, take her hand. "It's beautiful."

"Wait until you see the inside."

I walk her in and Irina comes to greet us, followed by Matteo. The smell of homemade bread wafts through the air and the rooms are bright with sunlight pouring in from the windows.

"It feels brighter," Amelia says.

She's right, it does, although physically, nothing has changed.

Matteo takes our bags and we walk into the living room.

"Are you hungry?" I ask.

Her gaze turns to the corridor that leads to the library. "No," she answers absently. "Not yet."

Irina nods, disappears into the kitchen.

"Come," I say, walking her toward the library.

She hesitates.

I turn to her, meet her cautious eyes. "It's all right."

She nods, lets me walk her into that corridor which is not as dark and not as cold anymore. I open the door to the library, and it's flooded with light and she smiles wide because I've replaced the dark stained glass with colors matching the restored garden fresco above our heads and we're bathed in soft blues and bright yellows and deep pinks.

Everything that was dark is now light.

The maze of bookshelves is cleared, the books

that could be salvaged, salvaged. Three walls make up the shelves now, all stacked high with books and instead of the single old armchair, there are two in here now. One for her and one for me.

"The door," she says, looking to where the door that led to the catacombs once was.

"It's sealed off. The shelves built into the wall."

She looks at me.

"Do you remember the crashing noise that day?"

That day.

She nods. She knows what day I mean.

"It was the stones giving way. The little girl's bones were buried behind them."

"What?"

"The little girl who lived here."

"Maybe that's where she was leading me all along. She wanted to be found."

"Maybe."

"Are you sure they were hers?"

"Yes. DNA. Hers and her puppy's. She's been buried beside her mother in a proper grave."

"I'm glad. I hope she's at peace."

She walks around the room, touches some of the spines of the books.

I watch her and I think about the light here and I think it has to do with her. I think she brings the light into this house.

Into my life.

I reach into my pocket and walk to her.

She puts the book she was looking at back and looks at me and she reads me so well now. Like she is so completely in tune with me. Like she's a part of me.

"What are you doing?" she asks with a smile.

I hold out my hand, open my palm.

Inside it lies a ring. A platinum band and diamonds surrounding a single perfect sapphire that pales beside her beautiful eyes.

The design is complicated and unique, like her.

She looks at it, touches her mouth with the fingers of one hand like she can't quite believe it, touches the band with the fingers of the other. She turns her pretty eyes to me, searches mine.

"I want to marry you," I say.

She laughs a strange nervous sort of giggle. Looks at the ring in my hand again.

I take her left hand, slide the ring onto her finger.

"Why?"

I look up at her, laugh with a shake of my head. "You ask the strangest questions at the strangest times."

She looks down at our hands and I seat the ring on her finger. It's a perfect fit.

I take her face in my hands and tilt it up. "Will you marry me, Amelia?"

A tear slides down her cheek but her mouth moves into a smile and she nods. "Yes. Yes, Gregory. I'll marry you."

EPILOGUE 1

SEBASTIAN

Christmas

My brother makes me out to be an asshole, but I'm just protecting what's mine. What's always been mine. He would have done the same if he stood in my shoes. And he will now with Amelia Willow.

But time does heal.

We're not close, Gregory and I, but we were never really close. Now that he has Amelia, though, everything is different. He's different. Not so anxious or wanting. Not so much on the outside, maybe.

"This thing's uncomfortable," Gregory says, stepping into the living room.

I look over at him and I have to agree. The tux *is* uncomfortable. I tug at the collar of mine.

"She won't eat if she hears you," Helena says. "Can't you go somewhere else?"

Gregory gives her a grin, walks over to where little Helena has just turned away from the bottle and is searching for her uncle. She smiles a huge smile as soon as she sees him.

"Nope," Gregory says.

I roll my eyes as Gregory reaches down to take the baby and the bottle.

She coos when Gregory tickles her neck and it's Helena's turn to roll her eyes.

"That's right, sweetheart. Your favorite uncle is here," Gregory taunts, taking a seat and slipping the bottle into her mouth. "Maybe you can spit up on my jacket so I have an excuse to take it off."

"Not happening. I have a backup. If I have to wear one, you have to wear one," I say, watching them together. Watching how Little Helena has her tiny hand on his chin and is staring up at him as she drinks her bottle.

He's watching her too, making faces. Silly ones. It's the strangest thing to see him like this.

Helena comes to me, perches on my lap, looks at them too, then turns to me to give me a warm smile, hugging her arm around my shoulders.

"It's weird," she whispers.

"I know." I wrap my arm around her waist.

It's Christmas day and we're gathered at Gregory's house just outside of Rome. And today is the wedding. And I'm happy for him. For both of them.

"You okay?" I ask Helena whose expression is more serious as she watches them.

She turns to me. "Yeah. Everything's just happened so fast. For us. For them. But it's okay. It's good."

Irina walks inside carrying Libby who's wide awake.

"I just fed her, but I think she wants her mama."

But when she walks toward us, Libby holds her arms out to me, her pretty little face beaming with a smile.

Helena stands as I take Libby, my smile widening when she grabs my cheeks. Helena leans down to give her a kiss on top of her head.

"I'd better get back to Amy," she says.

"We should head out soon."

"The priest will wait," Gregory says. "I'm paying him enough to do this today."

"I just want to be sure we're back in time to open the mountain of presents for the girls," I say, raising my eyebrows at him. "You realize this day is no different than any other day for them, right? I mean, they're too little to know it's Christmas or that their uncle spoils them."

"Don't look at me. That was all Amelia."

"Like her sister. Spoiling you all," I say to Libby,

tickling her nose with mine, trying to get her to let go of the fistful of hair she's got.

The girls are all dressed in pretty white dresses, ready for the ceremony. Charlotte and Samantha are still sleeping in their car seats.

I meet my brother's gaze when he shifts the baby onto his shoulder, setting the empty bottle aside and rubbing her back. She lays her head on him, content.

"Look at us," I say. "Never would have guessed this is where I'd be. Where we'd be."

Gregory smiles. "Tell me about it."

There's a quiet minute. "Are we good?" I ask.

We've never really talked about this. Talked about how he left. Talked about the contract I made him sign to keep him away from Helena before relinquishing my rights over his share of the inheritance.

"Yeah. We're good, brother," he says.

"I'm glad."

Little Helena lets out a tiny burp making us both smile as we hear the sound of heels clicking on the stairs. We walk to the edge of the living room and I glance at my brother as he first lays eyes on Amelia and my smile widens. I shift Libby into one arm and pat his back with my other hand.

He looks at me.

"Give her to me," I say, reaching my arm out for the baby. "Go get your girl."

He smiles, hands baby Helena over and turns his

gaze back to the stairs as Amelia descends, wearing a hand-made dress of white lace with long sleeves, a high neckline and generous floor-length skirt.

Helena follows close behind with the long veil collected in her arms.

She looks beautiful, they both do.

Once they get to the first floor and Gregory takes Amelia's hands, Helena comes to my side and she has tears in her eyes and a satisfied smile on her face.

I kiss her cheek. "I love you, you know that?" I whisper.

She glances up at me. "Never stop telling me that."

Irina comes to take the babies, and I take my wife in my arms.

EPILOGUE 2

GREGORY

The Gift

"You're not really supposed to see me before the wedding. It's bad luck," Amelia says once everyone's gone outside to strap the car seats in and we're alone in the house.

"I think you and I are overdue for good luck," I say, tucking a strand of blonde hair behind her ear. "You look beautiful." I pull her to me, liking the plunging back of the dress which is both demure and sensual all at once.

She blushes, glances away. "Thank you. And so do you."

"The tux is uncomfortable."

"Get over it."

I lean in to kiss her lightly on the lips. "I can't wait to get you out of that dress."

"Does your brain ever not go somewhere dirty?"

"Rarely."

The door opens and Sebastian peeks his head in. "You two ready?"

Amelia opens her mouth to respond, but I stop her. "We'll follow. You go ahead."

Sebastian takes a moment to study us, nods and disappears.

"We're going to be late," Amelia says.

"We're the main event. They'll wait."

I pull her into the living room, reach into the presents piled up for the girls and pick out the one I want. I hold it out to her.

"We're doing gifts after," she says, looking at it.

"Just one. This one's just for us, anyway."

She reaches out, takes it, gives me a strange look when she realizes it's just a rolled-up sheet of paper.

"What is it?"

"Open it."

She pulls on the ribbon to unwrap it slowly, peels away the decorative paper to unroll what's inside. She studies it, furrows her eyebrows and looks up at me.

"What is this?" she asks.

"Well," I say, turning the sheet so we're both looking at it. "This represents me—"

"But it's a partial skull."

"My dark side." I wink. "And this, this is you in case you weren't sure." But she should be because the eyes, they're perfect. And the way she's holding my face and kissing me, well, she should know. "The bird—"

"It's the same one I always see."

"A new beginning. Literally erasing the past."

"A tattoo?"

I nod. "Here," I touch the spot where the unfinished whipping post scene is at my back.

Tears fill her eyes and she looks from the sheet back to me, and when I pull her into my arms, I wipe away the teardrop that slips.

"Your makeup," I say, although I don't care if she has streaks of black running down her face. She'd still be the most beautiful woman I've ever laid eyes on.

"I love you so much, you know that?"

"I hope so, considering you're about to marry me." I say, trying to make light of it. I squeeze her closer. I swear I won't ever be close enough. Not with her. "I love you, Amelia. I can't imagine ever being without you. And I don't ever want you to look at me, at any part of me, and think you're not everything."

She lays her head on my shoulder, touches my cheek.

"Because you are. You are my everything."

The End.

EXCERPT FROM COLLATERAL

Charles steps aside and I walk hurriedly away, back into the house, past the soldier standing by the grand staircase and up toward my suite of rooms on the second floor, almost running by the time I reach the doors, wishing I could lock them, but I can't because the lock is on the outside.

I open both doors and walk inside, closing them behind me and leaning against them to catch my breath.

It takes me one moment to realize something is off.

The room is dark, the only light filtering from the party outside. The balcony doors are closed but I still hear the sound of five-hundred of my father's closest friends getting drunk on his dime. Well, my mother's dime, really.

But it's not that that's off. There's a smell that

doesn't belong here.

A look around tells me I'm alone. But the bedroom door, it's open. I know I'd closed it when I'd left.

I walk toward it. I don't make a sound.

No one should be up here. The soldier wouldn't have let anyone up.

I push the door wider and step inside. The smell, it's stronger in here and it's making me nauseous.

The room is too dark for me to see and I'm about to flip the light switch when a figure moves. Standing with his back to the windows, the light creates a sort of halo around him and he has the advantage. I can't see his face, but he can see mine in that same light.

I swallow, try to speak. "You're not supposed to be here," I finally manage, sensing something dangerous. And I remember for all the friends my father has bought, the number of his enemies is double that.

"No, I'm not," the man says, his voice a deep, sure timbre that ices my spine.

He takes a step forward and I take one back, my hand closing over the doorknob behind me.

Danger.

It ripples off him.

"What's that smell?" I ask before I can stop myself.

"Morgue," he answers, his voice low and hard.

He walks toward me, no hesitance in his step, and before I can move, he's standing just a few inches from me.

The smell clings to him and it's making me sick. When I cringe back, he leans toward me and I open my mouth to scream just as something clicks.

For a moment, I think it's a gun.

But then the room is bathed in soft, golden light. He'd just reached to switch on the lamp on the table beside me.

I exhale but my relief is short-lived.

The man is taller than my father. He's more than a foot taller than me and I'm wearing four-inch heels.

His disheveled hair is dark, eyes hazel and I think he's drunk. He must be. Only a drunk man would enter Gabriel Marchese's daughter's bedroom.

Or one with a death wish.

"Who are you?" I ask.

He doesn't answer me but studies my face instead. His eyes narrow as he takes me in, his gaze lowering to the swell of my breasts lifted and pushed together by this ridiculous gown. It, like the roses, is pink. A soft, champagne pink. A color I don't detest.

"I came with a gift," he says.

He tucks his hand into his pocket and for a moment, I wonder if he's going to pull out a knife or a gun. If he's going to kill me after all. Because I know this man is not my father's friend. Not even a business associate. And for the first time in my life, I think about the protection I've always lived under. The protection that often felt more stifling than anything else.

"It's your birthday, isn't it?" he asks, cocking his head to the side, setting one hand on the door above my head. He's leaning so close that I can feel the heat coming off his body.

I swallow.

"How did you get up here?" There are guards everywhere.

He lets what he's holding dangle and my gaze shifts to it, to the pendant hanging off a gold chain. It's too dark to make out the details.

"You shouldn't be up here. The party—"

"I'm not here for the party. I'm here for you, Gabriela."

My blood runs cold at his words.

My father, as much as I hate to admit it, scares me. But this man is terrifying.

His lips curve into something wicked. A grin. A sneer. I wonder if he can feel my fear. Maybe smell it coming off me. Men like this can, can't they?

"Turn around."

"Why?" I ask weakly.

"So I can give you your birthday present."

"I don't want—"

"I said turn around."

I should scream. Alert a guard. There are plenty

of them. But I just keep staring up into his hazel eyes and I think how strangely beautiful he is, even for as fucked up as he looks. As drunk as he obviously is. As crazed.

"Please just go," I manage.

"Turn. Around."

It's an order.

I swallow. Turn.

He moves his hand from above me once my back is to him, so when he lifts the chain over my head and brings it down to set the pendant against the swell of my breasts, I smell that smell again. On the sleeves of his suit. On the skin of his hands.

I look down at the pendant, but he pulls it higher so I can't see it. Instead, I notice the ring on his finger, a heavy, dark ring.

But then those fingers touch my skin and it's like touching a live wire. I gasp, listen to the hammering of my heart, wonder if he hears it. If he feels that shock of electricity.

I don't move as he pulls the chain tight, the pendant at my throat. He tugs and a new panic takes hold. I think he's going to strangle me with it.

I make a sound, a pathetic whimper. I should scream but it's like my throat has closed up.

"It's broken," he says. "That's rude, isn't it? To give you a broken gift?" His deep voice is low, his breath on my neck sending a strange sensation down my spine. "But that's how I got it, too."

I realize what he's doing. He's tying the chain. He must be.

I reach my hand to touch the pendant and when I do, something crusty flakes off.

A glance at my fingers shows a flake of dark red and I know it's blood. I know it.

My stomach heaves and I tighten my muscles, trying to quell the urge to vomit.

"There," he says. I smell whiskey on his breath now that he's closer and hear him inhale as the scruff of his jaw scratches my bare shoulder and I shudder.

Undeterred, he tilts my head to the side and presses his lips to the curve of my neck. To my pulse.

My breath catches and I can't move.

It's not a kiss, this.

This man isn't kissing me.

But his lips, they're warm. And that disgusting smell of chemicals and death, it's going to make me sick. He must feel my knees give out because he wraps one powerful, muscled arm around my middle, tightening his grip as he holds me against him.

He brings his mouth to my ear, breathes in a deep breath.

"Do you know who I am?" he asks in a whisper that makes the hair on the back of my neck stand on end.

I give a little shake of my head.

He turns me so I'm facing him, presses me against the door with one hand on my belly as the fingers of his other hand trail the line of my collarbone and touch the pendant.

When I finally meet his gaze, what I see in his eyes makes me go cold.

"Stefan Sabbioni," he says. "Antonio's brother."

Those names mean nothing to me. Should they mean something?

"And I want you to give your father a message for me," he starts, pausing for so long that it feels like the air is heavier for the unspoken words. For those that are still to come. "Tell him I'll be back to take something precious too."

An eternity passes before he steps backward.

My knees buckle, and I catch the doorknob to remain upright. It's suddenly freezing in my room and I'm shivering.

"You won't forget to give him my message, will you?"

I shake my head. It's all I can do.

He nods, eyes narrowing, a smile that's not a smile at all turning the corners of his mouth upward.

"Happy birthday, Gabriela," he says, and with that, he's gone.

Buy Collateral Now!

THANK YOU

Thank you for reading *Twisted!* I hope you enjoyed Gregory and Amelia's story. If you'd consider leaving a review at the store where you purchased this book, I would be so very grateful.

Make sure to sign up for my newsletter to stay updated on news and giveaways! You can find the link on my website: https://natasha-knight.com/subscribe/

Like my FB Author Page to keep updated on news and giveaways!

I have a FB Fan Group where I share exclusive teasers, giveaways and just fun stuff. Probably TMI :) It's called The Knight Spot. I'd love for you to join us!

ALSO BY NATASHA KNIGHT

Collateral Damage Duet

Collateral: an Arranged Marriage Mafia Romance

Damage: an Arranged Marriage Mafia Romance

Dark Legacy Trilogy

Taken (Dark Legacy, Book 1)
Torn (Dark Legacy, Book 2)
Twisted (Dark Legacy, Book 3)

MacLeod Brothers

Devil's Bargain

Benedetti Mafia World

Salvatore: a Dark Mafia Romance

Dominic: a Dark Mafia Romance

Sergio: a Dark Mafia Romance

The Benedetti Brothers Box Set (Contains Salvatore, Dominic and Sergio)

Killian: a Dark Mafia Romance

Giovanni: a Dark Mafia Romance

The Amado Brothers

Dishonorable

Disgraced

Unhinged

Standalone Dark Romance

Deviant

Beautiful Liar

Retribution

Theirs To Take

Captive, Mine

Alpha

Given to the Savage

Taken by the Beast

Claimed by the Beast

Captive's Desire

Protective Custody

Amy's Strict Doctor

Taming Emma

Taming Megan

Taming Naia

Reclaiming Sophie

The Firefighter's Girl

Dangerous Defiance

Her Rogue Knight

Taught To Kneel

Tamed: the Roark Brothers Trilogy

ACKNOWLEDGMENTS

Cover Design by CoverLuv

Cover Photography by Wander Aguiar

Cover Model Travis S.

Editing by Casey McKay

ABOUT THE AUTHOR

USA Today bestselling author of contemporary romance, Natasha Knight specializes in dark, tortured heroes. Happily-Ever-Afters are guaranteed, but she likes to put her characters through hell to get them there. She's evil like that.

Want more?
www.natasha-knight.com
natasha-knight@outlook.com